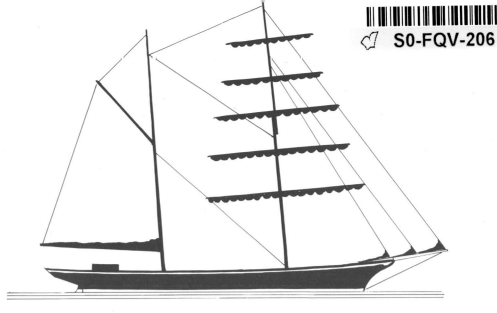

— BRIGANTINE —

Two masts, with the foremast square-rigged and the
mizzen-mast fore-&-aft rigged. A brig would set square sails on the
mizzen in addition to the fore-&-aft mainsail.

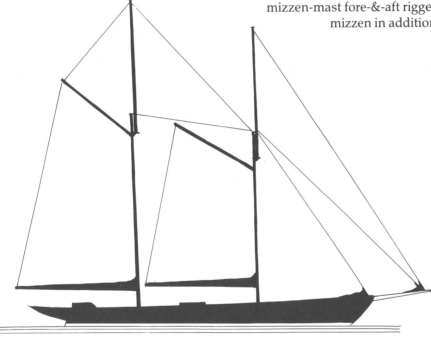

— SCHOONER —

Two or more masts, all fore-&-aft rigged, with the foremast shorter
than the mizzen-mast.

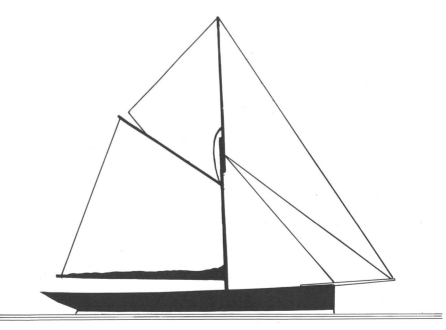

— CUTTER —

Single mast, either gaff- or bermudan- rigged, with two or more foresails.

TALL SHIPS
ON THE
HIGH SEAS

Beken of Cowes

TALL SHIPS
ON THE
HIGH SEAS

WITH A FOREWORD BY
HRH
THE PRINCE OF WALES

TEXT BY
Kenneth John Beken

WITH PHOTOGRAPHS BY
Frank William Beken
Alfred Keith Beken
Kenneth John Beken

E. P. DUTTON | NEW YORK

ACKNOWLEDGMENT

The authors wish to express
their grateful thanks to
Erik C. Abranson
for his invaluable help in
supplying information for
this book.

First published in 1985
by Harrap Ltd, London

First published in the
United States in 1986
by E. P. Dutton,
a division of
New American Library,
2 Park Avenue,
New York, N.Y. 10016.

Library of Congress
Catalog Card Number:
85-72940

ISBN: 0-525-24394-1

USA

DESIGNED BY MICHAEL R. CARTER

Colour origination
in Great Britain by
Peak Litho Plates
Tunbridge Wells

Printed and bound
in Italy by
G. Canale & C., Turin

10 9 8 7 6 5 4 3 2 1

First American Edition

CONTENTS

KENSINGTON PALACE

    There is something irresistibly romantic about large sailing ships which appeals to the vast majority of mankind. I remember reading about a recent gathering of tall ships - it may have been in Canada - where the organisers were overwhelmed by nearly a million people who wanted to come and see these beautiful maritime works of art. The paradox of our contemporary existence, with its constant emphasis on even more sophisticated technology and modes of transport, is that so many people develop an acute awareness of the value of our past and of such miracles of human ingenuity as these great ships, which have been so superbly illustrated in this book.

    The Beken family of Cowes, on the Isle of Wight, have been marine photographers for several generations and have been photographing successive generations of my family as we tacked up and down the Solent during Cowes Week. I feel sure that this book, so skilfully produced, will strike a seafaring chord in the hearts of many a true Briton and will remind us of the unique value these training ships can have as a kind of floating "initiation test" for today's young people. If only there were more of these elegant vessels......

Charles.

BEKEN OF COWES
A HISTORY

In the late 1880s, the family of Beken moved from Canterbury to Cowes, a small port on the north of the Isle of Wight. Frank Beken was then barely ten years old and, under the guidance of his father, a chemist, he started to experiment with photography. He was soon afloat in a dinghy, photographing the magnificent ships and yachts that graced the Solent area, with their beauteous and classical lines.

With his keen eye for composition, he made many a fine study of the early liners, steamers, square-riggers and schooners and later the 'J' class that attended and raced off Cowes, usually manned by visiting Royalty, nobility and other wealthy gentlemen. The art of Frank was repeated by his son Keith. Together they experimented with existing cameras, adapting them to their own special needs.

They could find no better cameras than the ones constructed by themselves to their own design — a wooden box with a ground glass viewfinder and a lens, the whole apparatus refined to their own special needs. These cameras used 8″ x 6″ glass plates and, over the past 100 years, a collection of over 50,000 fine negatives has been carefully stored and filed — a unique library. In 1970 Kenneth Beken joined his father and grandfather in the family company and for a short time, until the death of Frank, there were three generations making up 'Beken of Cowes'.

Each one of them, in turn, attained perhaps the highest honour in photography — a 'Fellowship of the Royal Photographic Society'. Beken of Cowes have the distinction of being 'by appointment to HRH The Duke of Edinburgh, marine photographers'.

In his early days, Frank Beken used only a dinghy, rowed by a competent oarsman, to negotiate his way through the biggest of the 300- and 400-ton schooners of 1890 vintage. Many years later he graduated to a steam launch, and then a petrol launch which had a maximum speed of eight knots, thus recording for posterity the passage of these great ships.

Keith Beken, his son, returning from his war years at sea, picked up his camera again and, with a somewhat faster launch, continued to build up their collection of

FRANK WILLIAM BEKEN   ALFRED KEITH BEKEN   KENNETH JOHN BEKEN

photographs of ships of the era. With an eye for colour photography, he then built his own camera to a 5″ x 4″ format. It was designed to stand up against rough seas and weather in general, factors which quickly destroy so many cameras.

It was not long before Kenneth Beken showed a flair for his family's work and found himself following in his father's footsteps. With the current world demand today for colour, in sport and action photographs, Kenneth now uses the modern medium-format cameras, such as the Rolleiflex 6006. With the help of a fast (35 knot) 'Boston Whaler' launch, and a helicopter for aerial work at sea, a further 50,000 2¼″-square colour transparencies have been added to this valuable collection of maritime history.

The Bekens depend upon the elements for their results — a critical factor. Rough weather and seas give fine pictures, but are enemies to the photographer who needs a stable platform for his camera. Light and shade are also all important, but are not always available.

Each 'Beken' works alone — in his own launch — so that he can concentrate on his subject without any distraction, for photographs often have to be taken in awkward and even dangerous circumstances; it is hardly necessary to add that each photographer has to be a 'man of the sea'.

This volume represents pictures of one hundred of the best 'Tall Ships', taken in locations which include Hawaii, Canada, the USA, the Caribbean, the Mediterranean and Europe, and Russia.

Included are the *Sedov*, the largest; to perhaps the smallest, *Fiddlers Green*. From the famous *Charlotte Rhodes* to the tragic *Marques* — each has her own story to tell.

Photograph by Colin Rogers Photomasters, Weymouth

INTRODUCTION

Her great sails bellied stiff, her great masts leaned,
They watched how the seas struck and burst, and greened.

The very name 'Tall Ships' creates in the imagination a vision of grace and beauty; yet, at the same time, an image of majesty and power as we remember the 'Cape Horners' battling their way around the great oceans of the world. Cresting these seas were the 'greyhounds', the clippers, such as *Cutty Sark* and *Thermopylae*, vying with each other to be the first home to Britain with the new tea crop. In those early days they flew over the seas as a bird goes — chartless; their crews revealed as passionate men at battle with the sea.

Gone now are such ships as the *Archibald Russell*, the *Pamir* and the *Passat*: ships of 5,000 tons and more, with a waterline length of over 300 feet, able to carry 4,000 tons of grain across thousands of miles of desolate ocean. Above those solid decks awash with green seas would stand four giant masts up to 200 feet above the keel, carrying a multitude of sails, adding up to 50,000 square feet of canvas with names to conjure with — Royals, topgallants, skysails and moonrakers. These were set on

GEORG STAGE 1956

HMS MARTIN

yards up to two feet thick, ninety feet in length and weighing up to five tons.

In the face of a sudden squall or approaching storm, the entire crew, down to the cook, would be sent aloft to gather in the thrashing canvas. The ships would roll thirty degrees to port, thirty degrees to starboard; and, in extreme latitudes, ice would fill the rigging, which meant that the crew had to chip it away to avoid a top-heavy ship capsizing onto her beam ends.

> *Their savage eyes, salt-reddened at the rims*
> *And icicles on their sou'wester brims.*

Round trips for these ships took months and even years. Ships would wait for cargoes to be negotiated; there would then be weeks of back-breaking loading and a lull before the trade winds arrived to spirit them homewards. Harsh discipline prevailed and creature comforts were few. Clothing and bedding would be at best damp, and at worst frozen solid.

It is a wonder today why men still dream of running away to sea. But then life afloat has changed to accommodate today's standards. The Tall Ships we see now would be regarded as luxury cruise ships by the men of yester-year.

The very term 'Tall Ships' has now been extended to encompass not only the square-rigged vessels of the last century, but cadet-training ships, luxury charter yachts and working merchantmen.

It is gratifying that navies, corporate groups, and even private individuals still

Opposite page
PASSAT

13

regard Tall Ships as being worth the capital required — many thousands of pounds — to keep them afloat; for as working cargo carriers their financial return is limited.

After the introduction of steam power at the beginning of the nineteenth century, the bulk-carrying square-riggers continued to hold their own for a number of years. Motor power was understandably unreliable, but the first successful crossing of the Atlantic under auxiliary steam power was accomplished by the *Savannah* in 1819. Although the days of sail power then began to wane, it was not until some fifty years later, with the opening of the Suez Canal, that commerical sailing ships realized they could no longer compete with steam.

To ease costs, crews were often made up with trainee cadets. Up to the Second World War, those sailing bulk carriers that still remained would often train cadets who were ultimately destined for merchant and military naval careers. Even today, many navies still insist that a 'spell before the mast' is essential as basic training and character building for their cadets. Since the Second World War most of these training ships have been purpose built for their roles. Many are converted bulk carriers, such as *Kruzenshtern* and *Sedov*; others, such as *Dar Mlodziezy* and *Simon Bolivar*, were especially commissioned, to designs of early working vessels, as passenger carriers for training purposes only.

With each country showing great pride in owning its own Tall Ship it was a natural progression for them to meet, with a view to friendly competition and international exchange. Thus it was in 1956 that the Sail Training Association of Great Britain held their first Tall Ships Race from Torbay in England to Lisbon in Portugal, some 760 miles.

The race was an immediate success and since that time, approximately every two years, sail training events have taken place all over the world. Interest in sail

MERCATOR

training is still very strong, with new ships being commissioned and launched, adding to or replacing those which have been lost. These ships are rarely allowed to fade away; they are loved and cherished and in their retiring years are often preserved as museum ships or commercial exhibits.

Thus, not only are we presented with a ship in mid-ocean, under full sail with a 'bone between her teeth', but we may also wander to our heart's content over such ships that have been preserved and opened to the public. We have seen the young people of today, of both sexes and sixteen or seventeen years old, strung out on the yards — 'the flying topsails thundering like a drum, battling the gale that makes men dumb'. So to them we say:

> *Adventure on, and if you suffer, swear,*
> *That the next adventurer shall have less to bear:*
> *Your way will be retrodden — make it fair.*

We are indebted to Her Majesty's Customs & Excise for the reproduction of this letter which was in fact sent to them in 1790. The writer of the letter was presumably in such a fury that he dated it incorrectly.

To Captain Bursack on board Speedwell Revenue
Cutter now lying at

Sir /

Damn thee

and God damn thy two Purblind Eyes thou Buger and thou Death
looking Son of a Bitch O that I had bin there (with my company) for
thy Sake when thou tookes them Men of Mine on Board the Speedwell
Cutter on Monday 4 Decr. I would drove thee and all thy Gang to Hell
where thou Belongest thou Devil Incarnet. Go Down thou Hell Hound into
thy Kennell below and Bathe thy Self in that Sulphurous Lake that has
bin so long Prepared for such as thee for it is time the World was rid of
such a Monster thou art no Man but a Devil thou fiend. O Lucifer I
hope that thou will soon fall into Hell like a Star from the Sky; there to lie
(unpitied) and unrelented of any for Ever & Ever. Which God Grant of his
Infinite Mercy. Amen.
                                                                    J.Spurier

Fordingbridge.Jan: 32, 1700 & fast asleep

AMERICA

In 1851 a fast schooner named the *America* arrived at Cowes on the Isle of Wight. The best British yachts were mustered to challenge her in a race around the Island set for 22 August, the distance to be just under sixty miles and the prize 'the Hundred Guinea Trophy'; *America* won by eighteen minutes and took the cup back to the United States. The trophy has since been re-named The America's Cup and has prompted the spending of many millions of pounds in trying to wrench it away from the New York Yacht Club, where it lay until 1983 when *Australia II* won that coveted prize.

In 1966 Rudolf J. Schaeffer commemorated the 125th anniversary of the founding of his company, Schaeffer Breweries', by building a replica of that legendary yacht. Referring to plans held by the British Admiralty, who had them drawn when the original yacht was under British ownership, Sparkman & Stevens, the American yacht designers, drew the lines for the new schooner. She was traditionally built of pine using period tools and, although up-to-date below decks, was near identical to the original in other respects. Even the sails were made by Ratsey & Lapthorn, who had supplied the original yacht with a jib some 115 years previously.

In 1979 the *America II* was sold to Senor Carlos Perdomo. She was sold again in 1981 and is currently under the ownership of Spaniard Ramon Mendoza. Although now painted white, she is shown in this picture in her original livery of high gloss black.

Name of vessel	America
Year launched	1967
Designer	George Steers, William Brown and Sparkman & Stevens
Builder	Goudy & Steven, East Boothbay, Maine, USA
Current owner	Ramon Mendoza
Current flag	Spain
Rig	Two-masted gaff schooner
Construction	Wood
Length overall	130 feet
Length of hull	104.8 feet
Length waterline	90.7 feet
Beam	22.8 feet
Draught	11.5 feet
Tonnage	92.24 gross; 165.5 displ; 190 TM
Sail area	5,387 sq. feet
Engines	2 x 320 bhp GM 8V-71 diesels
Photograph date	1968
Photograph location	Cowes, England

AMERIGO VESPUCCI

Based at La Spezia in Italy, the *Amerigo Vespucci* is the largest sailing vessel in the Mediterranean. Her striking looks make an impressive sight reminiscent of a nineteenth-century man-o-war. Compared with her contemporaries, she is more 'short and wide' than 'long and thin', though her very long bowsprit and her tall, narrow rig balance her proportions. One hundred and fifty cadets from the Laghorn Naval Academy train on static masts rigged to match those on *Amerigo Vespucci*, prior to their five-month cruise. The only thing that cannot be simulated is the ship's roll!

Designed to accommodate these 150 cadets within a fixed hull length, *Amerigo Vespucci* has three full decks above sea level plus a long poop deck. Her name is taken from the noted Italian merchant navigator who also gave his name to the Americas. Indeed, *Amerigo Vespucci* herself has visited both North and South America on her travels, though she usually cruises in the Mediterranean and along European coasts. There was once a sister-ship, the *Christoforo Colombo*, taken by the Russians in 1945 as a war prize. Re-named *Dunay*, she was eventually scrapped in 1972.

The *Amerigo Vespucci* has attended a number of sail training events, but as a spectator only — due to her limited racing ability. On deck though she is truly spectacular. Four huge wooden wheels on one shaft are used to steer her and each halyard, sheet and belaying pin is labelled with a brass plate. She is pictured here off Cowes during a courtesy visit to the 1977 Cowes Week Yacht Regatta.

Name of vessel	Amerigo Vespucci
Year launched	1931
Designer	Francesco Rotundi
Builder	Castellamare Di Stabia Shipyard, Naples, Italy
Current owner	Italian Navy
Current flag	Italy
Rig	Three-masted full-rigged ship
Construction	Steel
Length overall	331.6 feet
Length of hull	269.2 feet
Beam	51.2 feet
Draught	24 feet
Tonnage	4,100 load displ; 2,686 TM
Sail area	32,300 sq. feet
Engines	2 x 950 Fiat diesels
Photograph date	1977
Photograph location	Cowes, England

AMPHITRITE

Amphitrite was built as a private yacht for Colonel MacGregor, the then Viceroy of India. Launched in 1887 under her original name of *Hinemoa*, she was solidly built of teak and rigged as a schooner to be used for extended cruising.

She was successively owned by the Earl of Harewood and the Earl of Arran prior to being bought by a Swedish gentleman named Hans Ostermann. He rigged her as a barquentine and re-named her *Amphitrite*. In 1969 she was sold to the French Port Grimaud property real estate promoter M. Francois Spoerry. He kept her for five years, selling her on to the Horst Film GmbH of Berlin who used her in the making of two films about the ships *Mary Celeste* and the *Niobe*. In 1975 she passed into the ownership of the Clipper-Deutsches Jugendwerk Zur See. She underwent an extensive refit and her rig was changed to that of a gaff schooner with foreyard.

She now has a crew of six, training twenty-two youngsters on cruises around the Baltic, and is one of the oldest training ships in service today. Our photograph shows her leaving Marseilles harbour under shortened sail as she runs with the Mistral wind.

Name of vessel	Amphitrite
Year launched	1887
Designer	Camper & Nicholson
Builder	Camper & Nicholson, Gosport, England
Current owner	Clipper-Deutsches Jugendwerk Zur See e.V
Current flag	Federal Republic of Germany
Rig	Three-masted barquentine
Construction	Wood
Length overall	139.1 feet
Length waterline	107 feet
Beam	18.8 feet
Draught	12.1 feet
Tonnage	111 gross; 161 TM
Sail area	8,250 sq. feet
Engines	2 x 365 bhp Daimler-Benz diesels
Photograph date	1967
Photograph location	Marseilles, France

AQUILA MARINA

Hans Petersen, a shipowner from Marstal, Denmark, had this oak-hulled schooner built in 1920 at Nyborg and she was launched under the name *Als*. She was a working ship and sailed un-engined on coastal trading routes in the Baltic and North European ports. In 1923 she was sold to Alexander Persson of Sweden. Re-named *Elsa*, she was fitted with a 60 bhp auxiliary engine in 1926 and was a working vessel until 1965 when she was sold out of trade to Messrs P. Holt and P. Wickers in England. She was based at Gillingham and used for fishing parties by tourists. Five years later she was bought by fellow Briton Mr P. Gaskell-Brown, of the Plymouth Sailing School, and during that time she appeared in the famous television series the *Onedin Line*.

She is now under the ownership of Jochen Mass, the noted German racing driver. Fitted-out as a comfortable charter vessel for 8 guests, she operated out of Villefranche and Monte Carlo while spending time in the West Indies and Baltic area. This picture was taken of her when she attended a sail parade in Quebec in 1984.

Name of vessel	Aquila Marina
Year launched	1920
Builder	Built at Nyborg, Denmark
Current owner	The Windship Corporation, Guernsey, Channel Islands
Current flag	Great Britain
Rig	Three-masted topsail schooner
Construction	Wood
Length overall	124.8 feet
Length of hull	98.8 feet
Length waterline	98.5 feet
Beam	25 feet
Draught	9.2 feet
Tonnage	100 gross; 180 displ; 191 TM
Sail area	6,040 sq. feet
Engines	1 x 140 bhp 6 cylinder Albin diesel
Photograph date	1984
Photograph location	Quebec, Canada

ARIADNE

This vessel started life as a Dutch three-masted auxiliary schooner trading around the north and western coast of Africa. She was originally named the *San Antonio* and for thirty years was a successful merchantman.

After the Second World War she earned her keep trading around the Baltic under the Swedish flag bearing the names *Santoni,* and later *Buddy,* until she was purchased by the German Captain Paschburg in 1973. She was given a complete refit, with the emphasis on luxury passenger cruising, and she can now accommodate forty-six persons in eighteen cabins. Eleven crew were used to man the ship and she was chartered in the West Indies and the Mediterranean.

In 1971 she was used as support ship for the German Admiral's Cup Team campaigning three ocean racing yachts off Cowes, and our picture was taken then on one sunny afternoon in August.

In 1979 she was bought by the French sailing holiday company Mondovoile, of Paris, but after three years she was sold to the German Schulschiffverein 'Grossherzogin Elisabeth' e.V. She now bears the name *Grossherzogin Elisabeth* in memory of an earlier training ship, and she is run by a Merchant Navy school training stewards and cooks for sea duties. During the summer months she undertakes some cruises together with some charter work, so she is still appreciated and well used.

Name of vessel	Ariadne
Year launched	1909
Builder	Jan Smit, Ablasserdam, Holland
Current owner	Schulschiffverein 'Grossherzogin Elisabeth' e.V
Current flag	Federal Republic of Germany
Rig	Three-masted foreyard schooner
Construction	Steel
Length overall	209.1 feet
Length of hull	151 feet
Beam	27 feet
Draught	9.8 feet
Tonnage	462 gross
Sail area	10,800 sq. feet
Engines	1 x 400 bhp Caterpillar diesel
Photograph date	1977
Photograph location	Cowes, England

ARTEMIS

The *Artemis* was built in 1902 at the yard of Zacharias T. Jacobsen in Torense, Denmark and launched in January 1903 as the *Noah*. For many years she traded across the Baltic, the North Sea, to England, France, Germany, Iceland, Italy, Africa, Newfoundland and all the places where a large trading schooner could still find a cargo. She mainly carried salt and timber, but also salt fish, bricks, coal, china, clay, wheat and sundry commodities.

In 1930 she was fitted with her first engine, a 110 bhp diesel, and fifteen years later she passed into the hands of new owners who re-named her *Peder Most*, registering her in Svendborg. She was though almost immediately re-sold to become the *Anna Thora* of Aalborg. Re-sold again in 1946, she became the *Thora*. By that time she was engaged in local coastal trading and her rig was reduced to suit. In 1947 she was sold to H. Jeppesen and became the *Artemis* of Copenhagen.

Between the years 1954 and 1965 she was owned by a Marstal syndicate who used her as a motorized coaster. Then she was bought by Captain Nicholas Dekker who registered her in Rotterdam. He restored her to a three-masted schooner with a single deep topsail. The idea was to transport antiques in her hold and offer them for sale at various ports, but red tape and customs bureaucracy made things difficult. In 1976 Nicholas Dekker entered *Artemis* in the Tall Ships Race from Plymouth (where we photographed her) to New York with the intention of selling her in the USA. *Artemis* was bought by Rick and Sharron Harrington of Texas who made her into a mobile maritime museum based in Galveston and Mobile. This venture was not a financial success and *Artemis* was sold once more to Anglo-Canadian Chris Guiry in 1979.

On 5 May 1980 she left Mobile, Alabama bound for Canada with eight crew and a cargo of wood-burning stoves. In the early hours of 9 May she was struck by a vicious storm with squalls that twice knocked her down. Her pumps could not handle water taken in due to a leak below the waterline, and *Artemis* sank by nightfall. Fortunately the crew were all saved.

Name of vessel	Artemis
Year launched	1903
Designer	Z.T. Jacobsen
Builder	Z.T. Jacobsen, Troense, Denmark
Current owner	Schooner Ventures, Canada
Current flag	Canada
Rig	Three-masted schooner
Construction	Wood
Length overall	147.7 feet
Length of hull	120 feet
Length waterline	106 feet
Beam	25.9 feet
Draught	10.2 feet
Tonnage	240 gross; 380 displ; 284 TM
Sail area	6,027 sq. feet
Engines	1 x 120 bhp Burmeister & Wain Alpha diesel
Photograph date	1976
Photograph location	Plymouth, England

ASGARD II

This fine emerald green brigantine was especially commissioned to replace the ageing *Asgard I*, a Colin Archer gaff-rigged ketch. The original vessel was built in 1905 and purchased from Erskine Childers by the Irish Sail Training Association, 'the Coiste an Asgard', in 1964.

By 1975, the old *Asgard* had outlived her usefulness and plans were made to replace her with a new purpose-built vessel. She was laid up, and now preserved, with the sailing duties carried out by the bermudan ketch *Creidne*. *Asgard II* took to the seas in 1981 and, although owned by the 'Coiste an Asgard', she is managed by the state-owned company 'Irish Shipping Ltd' of Dublin. Her crew of five take twenty boys and girls on adventure training cruises, of two weeks duration, around the Irish and European coasts. The emphasis is on character building.

She is shown here shaking off a brisk nor'-westerly in the Solent off Cowes at the end of the 1982 Tall Ships Race from Vigo in Spain to Southampton. Her figurehead is that of Grainne Mhaol, a noted female captain from sixteenth-century Irish history.

Name of vessel	Asgard II
Year launched	1981
Designer	John Tyrell
Builder	Tyrell & Sons, Wicklow, Ireland
Current owner	Coiste an Asgard, Ireland
Current flag	Eire
Rig	Two-masted brigantine
Construction	Wood
Length overall	99 feet
Length of hull	84 feet
Length waterline	70 feet
Beam	21 feet
Draught	9.5 feet
Tonnage	92.67 gross; 120 TM
Sail area	4,000 sq. feet
Engines	1 x 160 bhp Kelvin Marine diesel
Photograph date	1982
Photograph location	Cowes, England

BARBA NEGRA

This ship is reported to have started life as a whaler out of Norway. Unlike the *Essex* (See later) she still sails today though in a different role; that of a research vessel to save the whales! At the start of the twentieth century she was employed carrying fish and general cargo, and remained in trade until 1956. Her current owners, Captains A. Seidl and G. Schwisow, purchased her in 1970 and renovated her completely for chartering in the West Indies. She has even played host to the famous French diver Jacques Cousteau on one of his research trips, although *Barba Negra* is pictured here undertaking a sail training role.

She visited England in 1974 and took part in the Royal Review past *HMY Britannia* in the Solent off Cowes. She later took part in New York's OPSAIL '76 and, when sail training, she carries nine officers and ten cadets.

Name of vessel	Barba Negra
Year launched	1896
Designer	John Lekve
Builder	Built in Norway
Current owner	Captains Albert Seidl & G. Schwisow, Canada
Current flag	Canada
Rig	Three-masted barquentine
Construction	Wood
Length overall	110 feet
Length waterline	79 feet
Beam	21 feet
Draught	12 feet
Tonnage	55.64 gross; 123 TM
Sail area	4,300 sq. feet
Engines	1 x 230 bhp Scania diesel
Photograph date	1974
Photograph location	Cowes, England

BEL ESPOIR II

This vessel was launched in 1944 as the auxiliary three-mast foreyard schooner *Nette S.* of Svendborg. In 1946 she was transferred from her owner A.E. Sørensen to his son M.H. Sørensen, and re-named *Peder Most*. In 1951 she was put into trade with Greenland and converted to carry cattle in 1953. On the short run from Copenhagen to Hamburg she could carry 200 head.

In 1955 she was bought by the Moray Sea School of the Outward Bound Trust, at Burghead, Scotland, as a replacement for the ageing *Prince Louis* (which had been on loan to the trust from Gordonstoun School). She was then re-named *Prince Louis II* and fitted out for five crew and twenty-four youngsters. For the next thirteen years she sailed around the Scottish coast until sold in 1968 to the Paris-based association 'Les Amis de Jeudi-Dimanche'. This is a juvenile delinquent rehabilitation society run by the Jesuit, Michael Jaouen.

Now known as *Bel Espoir II*, she has to spend most of her time on charter due to lack of funds. Fitted out for thirty trainees or passengers, she has a regular crew of six to eight. Based at Le Havre in France, she sails to the West Indies in winter and Europe in the summer months.

Name of vessel	Bel Espoir II
Year launched	1944
Designer	J. Ring Andersen
Builder	J. Ring Andersen, Svenborg, Denmark
Current owner	Les Amis de Jeudi-Dimanche, Paris, France
Current flag	France
Rig	Three-masted topsail schooner
Construction	Wood
Length overall	126.3 feet
Length of hull	96 feet
Length waterline	90 feet
Beam	23.3 feet
Draught	9.8 feet
Tonnage	99 gross; 130 displ; 183 TM
Sail area	7,000 sq. feet
Engines	1 x 288 bhp Baudoin diesel
Photograph date	1975
Photograph location	River Thames, London

BELLE BLONDE

This ship was originally built as the staysail rigged schooner lightship number 88 for the United States Coast Guard. She was fitted with a steam engine and spent most of her working life off Astoria, Oregon. This necessitated a trip around Cape Horn which she apparently managed without mishap.

In 1962 she was given to the Columbia River Maritime Museum in Astoria and her current owner purchased her in October 1982. Captain Lacerte had already built and chartered a 135-feet barquentine in the Pacific and he set about the complete renovation of his new aquisition the *Belle Blonde III*, in Victoria, B.C., Canada. She was completed in time to race in company with other Tall Ships from San Juan to Bermuda and then on to Halifax in Canada.

She has a sister-ship preserved at New York's Maritime Museum, though *Belle Blonde* is unique as a working representation of a vessel of her type. Our photograph was taken at the start of the Bermuda to Halifax race (which marked the loss of the *Marques*) in June 1984.

Name of vessel	Belle Blonde
Year launched	1906
Builder	Built at Newark, New Jersey, USA
Current owner	Claude Lacerte, Canada
Current flag	Canada
Rig	Two-masted brigantine
Construction	Iron hull ⅝" and 3½" wood decks
Length overall	165 feet
Length of hull	135 feet
Length waterline	129 feet
Beam	30 feet
Draught	14 feet
Tonnage	478 gross; 276 net
Sail area	14,000 sq. feet
Engines	1 x Washington diesel 350 bhp
Photograph date	1984
Photograph location	Bermuda

BELLE POULE

The *Belle Poule* and her sister-ship *Etoile* were built for the French Navy as training ships, but their hulls and rigs are taken from the turn-of-the-century Breton fishing schooners. Based at Paimpol and other Channel ports, they would fish off Iceland and were known as Icelandic schooners.

Sturdy, seaworthy craft, they were built to withstand North Atlantic gales yet have easily managed sails, as their purpose was to go fishing not sailing. Each carries seventeen permanent officers and crew who train twenty cadets. These cadets are midshipmen from Lanvéoc-Poulmic Naval College, near Brest, together with some reserve naval officers. Cruises seldom venture far afield from home shores and vary from four to fourteen days. *Belle Poule* was on a visit to the south coast of England when this picture was taken in the Solent in a typical August south-westerly.

Name of vessel	Belle Poule
Year launched	1932
Designer	Chantiers Navals de Normandie
Builder	Chantiers Navals de Normandie, Fecamp, France
Current owner	Lanvéoc-Poulmic Naval College, France
Current flag	France
Rig	Two-masted topsail schooner
Construction	Wood
Length overall	123 feet
Length of hull	106.1 feet
Length waterline	83 feet
Beam	24.6 feet
Draught	11.5 feet
Tonnage	275 displ; 227 TM
Sail area	4,570 sq. feet
Engines	1 x 300 bhp diesel
Photograph date	1982
Photograph location	Cowes, England

BILL OF RIGHTS

Newport, Rhode Island is the home of many a fine yacht, and among them is the *Bill of Rights.* She is a faithful replica of an 1856 gaff schooner even to her lack of an engine. She has however, six watertight bulkheads, emergency lighting, lifeboats and modern radio and navigational equipment.

She was built essentially for the holiday passenger trade but some of her time is earmarked for training purposes. Thirty-two youngsters can be carried, aged between fifteen and twenty-five, and three berths a month are set aside for sixteen to twenty-two year-olds who are interested in learning seamanship skills. *Bill of Rights* is manned by a crew of eight with passengers accommodated in eleven two-berth cabins, one three-berth, one four-berth and three single-berth cabins. Her cruises usually run from two to seven days, predominantly off New England.

Bill of Rights cuts a fine sight here as she sails through the fairway of Newport Harbour, Rhode Island, on her way to New York for their Tall Ship gathering 'Operation Sail 1976'.

Name of vessel	Bill of Rights
Year launched	1971
Designer	McCurdy & Rhodes and Bates
Builder	Harvey F. Gamage, South Bristol, Maine, USA
Current owner	Joseph M. Davis Jnr USA
Current flag	United States of America
Rig	Two-masted gaff schooner
Construction	Wood
Length overall	151 feet
Length of hull	125 feet
Length waterline	85 feet
Beam	24.5 feet
Draught	10.5 feet
Tonnage	99.32 gross; 160 displ.
Sail area	6,300 sq. feet
Engines	none
Photograph date	1976
Photograph location	Newport, Rhode Island, USA

BLACK PEARL

This small brigantine was built by C. Lincoln Vaughn as his private yacht and he used her for cruises along the American east coast. She was purchased in 1959 by Barclay H. Warburton III who was to found the American Sail Training Association in 1973, and become its first president. *Black Pearl* was used for six years until 1966 for cruising in the Bahamas and between the West Indies and Nova Scotia. During that time youngsters often undertook tuition aboard. In 1964 she was the only private vessel in New York's OPSAIL and carried five training cadets.

In 1972 she took part in the Tall Ships Race from Cowes to the Baltic, breaking a long tradition of non-participation by USA vessels, and she is pictured here off Kiel. She was joined in that race by the US Coast Guard barque *Eagle*, and it was the success of this visit that inspired Warburton to set up an American Sail Training Organization. This association organized the final legs of the 1976 Tall Ships Race between Bermuda, Newport and New York, and *Black Pearl* participated under the command of Warburton's son, Barclay Warburton IV. *Black Pearl* has accommodation for up to ten persons with a four-berth foc's'le, two double cabins and a double master cabin.

Barclay Warburton III was very much in love with *Black Pearl* and took to permanent living on board towards the end of his life. He died prematurely in 1983 and bequeathed her to the American Sail Training Association. However they were not geared up to run her, mainly due to lack of funds. Overdue repairs were completed and she was put up for sale. In 1984 she was bought by the South Street Seaport Museum, of New York City, for $75,000. She will still be used for training cruises plus an annual one month charter to the American Sail Training Association for $1.

Name of vessel	Black Pearl
Year launched	1951
Designer	Edson Shock
Builder	C.L. Vaughn, Wickford, Rhode Island, USA
Current owner	South Street Seaport Museum, New York
Current flag	United States of America
Rig	Two-masted brigantine
Construction	Wood
Length overall	69.5 feet
Length of hull	59 feet
Length waterline	41.5 feet
Beam	15.5 feet
Draught	8.2 feet
Tonnage	27 gross; 36 displ; 41 TM
Sail area	1,991 sq. feet
Engines	1 x 165 bhp Hercules diesel
Photograph date	1972
Photograph location	Kiel, Germany

BLUENOSE II

The original *Bluenose* was built in 1921 as a Grand Banks racing-fishing schooner to challenge for the International Fisherman's Trophy. The *Bluenose*, which bore the nickname of the inhabitants of Nova Scotia, won the cup back from the Americans, and despite the many Canadian and American schooners built to beat her, retained the cup for the whole of her twenty-year racing history. She became a symbol of national pride and featured on Canadian stamps and she is still to be seen on the reverse side of Canadian 10-cent coins (dimes).

In 1942, when every available ship was pressed into the war effort, she was sold to a West Indian company for freighting in southern waters. Unfortunately she was wrecked on a reef off Haiti on 29 January 1946.

Bluenose II was ordered as an exact replica by the Halifax Company Oland & Son Ltd. She was built by Smith & Rhuland in Lunenburg, the same yard which had built the original schooner — even some of the men had worked on the original! Launched on 23 July 1963, she only needs a crew of fourteen, instead of the original twenty-nine, as there are various modern sailing aids aboard — such as hydraulics for raising anchor and sails. Accommodation is set for twelve persons and she has auxiliary engines and modern navigational equipment.

After eight years in the charter trade, she was transferred for $1 to the Province of Nova Scotia and she now fulfils a role as prestigious ambassador. Normally operating on one-day cruises out of Halifax, she also undertakes longer cruises on special charters and promotions, but no racing. She has attended a number of special Tall Ship events, including the Canadian Windjammer Rally in 1974, New York's OPSAIL '76, Quebec's parade in 1984 and here, as we have shown her, at Philadelphia on the Delaware in 1982.

Name of vessel	Bluenose II
Year launched	1963
Designer	William Roue
Builder	Smith & Rhuland Ltd., Lunenburg, Nova Scotia, Canada
Current owner	Dept. of Tourism, Nova Scotia
Current flag	Canada
Rig	Two-masted gaff schooner
Construction	Wood
Length overall	160 feet
Length of hull	143 feet
Length waterline	112 feet
Beam	27 feet
Draught	15.8 feet
Tonnage	191 gross; 285 displ.
Sail area	11,690 sq. feet
Engines	2 x 180 bhp diesels
Photograph date	1982
Photograph location	Philadelphia, USA

CABBY

The *Cabby* was the last full-size Thames Spritsail barge ever to be built of wood. Commissioned by the London & Rochester Trading Co., at Friensbury near Rochester, Kent, she is still owned by that company which now trades under the name Crescent Shipping. Their fleet consists of forty-four ships, trading between Spain and Sweden, and contains some motor barges; a few of these were original sailing barges like *Cabby*, but only she has been restored to sail. She was built as a general cargo carrier for the south-eastern areas of England, and after the fitting of her first engine in 1949 she was soon cut down to a motor barge.

Re-rigged in the 1970s, she now operates as a charter vessel for promotional cruises, receptions and conferences. The hold has been kept clear and is not divided into cabins, the accommodation for twelve persons being swinging hammocks. For a number of years she was under contract to Bell's Scotch Whisky and displayed their logo on her sails, the idea being a traditional way of advertising. Promoting this product always made her welcome at any port, especially in the Solent during Cowes Week when this photograph was taken!

Name of vessel	Cabby
Year launched	1928
Builder	London & Rochester Trading Co. Friensbury, Kent, England
Current owner	Crescent Shipping, UK
Current flag	Great Britain
Rig	Thames sailing spritsail barge
Construction	Wood
Length overall	91.6 feet
Beam	21.6 feet
Draught	7.3 feet
Tonnage	96.35 gross
Engines	1 x 65 bhp Kelvin K4 diesel
Photograph date	1976
Photograph location	Cowes, England

CAPTAIN SCOTT

Now owned by the Sultan of Oman and re-named *Shabab Oman* (meaning Youth of Oman) the *Captain Scott* was launched in 1971 for the Dulverton Trust. Closely linked with the Outward Bound Trust, her task was to take youngsters on adventure training courses to instil a spirit of adventure and initiative. As a replacement for the *Prince Louis II* sold in 1966 and now called *Bel Espoir II*, *Captain Scott* was a perfect vessel.

Her permanent crew of eight, together with three extra officers, would take thirty-six trainees on month-long courses around the north coasts of Scotland and Ireland. They were taught all aspects of seamanship plus onshore activities such as rock climbing and ornithology. *Captain Scott* could stay offshore in all but the very worst weather conditions and courses on board counted towards the Duke of Edinburgh Award Scheme. Her name was taken from the famous Captain Robert Falcon Scott of Antarctica and for six years was extensively used in her training role.

However, due to economical reasons and running costs she was put up for sale and purchased for use in the Middle East. Now painted white, she sails the Indian Ocean training cadets from the Omani Armed Forces under the management of the Omani Navy. Our view of her was taken in 1972 in her original livery when she visited Cowes for the Sail Training Race to the Skaw. In the background can be seen the US barque *Eagle* before her red Coast Guard stripe was added.

Name of vessel	Captain Scott
Year launched	1971
Designer	Robert Clark, Cmdr Victor Clark & Capt Michael Willoughby
Builder	Herd & MacKenzie, Buckie, Scotland
Current owner	Sultan of Oman
Current flag	Oman
Rig	Three-masted topgallant schooner
Construction	Wood
Length overall	171 feet
Length of hull	144.2 feet
Length waterline	129 feet
Beam	28 feet
Draught	15 feet
Tonnage	264.35 gross; 380 displ; 460 TM
Sail area	9,097 sq. feet
Engines	2 x 230 Gardner diesels
Photograph date	1972
Photograph location	Cowes, England

CARIAD

Cariad was built as a cruising yacht for Lord Dunraven. He had made his name with the yachts *Valkyrie II and III* which challenged for the America's Cup in 1893 and 1895 respectively. After a rather ignominious defeat which left both sides arguing, Lord Dunraven commissioned the firm of Summers & Payne to design and build him a fast cruising ketch. In 1896 she was launched into Southampton Water. During his ownership, she won a number of races and was even chartered to Richard D'Oyly Carte for a cruise.

1901 though saw her under new owners, and she changed hands a number of times and encompassed three round the world cruises. She underwent a major refit in Antigua in 1982 and in 1983 she returned home to the Solent. Her rig was reduced in the 1950s from 5,480 square feet to 4,500 square feet of sail. This affected her performance somewhat although, as we can see from the photograph, she makes a splendid sight nearly ninety years after her launch.

She was the centre of attention during the 1983 Cowes Week when she sailed through the Solent in company with the very latest Admirals Cup yachts, showing them that for all their speed and manoeuverability they could not match this yacht for grace and beauty. She is currently engaged in charter work in the Mediterranean.

Name of vessel	Cariad
Year launched	1896
Designer	Payne
Builder	Summers & Payne, Southampton, England
Current flag	British Virgin Islands
Rig	Two-masted gaff ketch
Construction	Wood on steel
Length overall	118 feet
Length of hull	106 feet
Length waterline	81 feet
Beam	18.5 feet
Draught	11.5 feet
Tonnage	129 TM
Sail area	4,500 sq. feet
Engines	1 x 320 bhp General Motors diesel
Photograph date	1983
Photograph location	Cowes, England

CHARLOTTE RHODES

Perhaps the most famous Tall Ship now, thanks to a starring role in TV's *Onedin Line*, the *Charlotte Rhodes* started life as the *Christian* and was the first Danish-built three-master to be supplied with an auxiliary engine. The advent of motor power heralded a time when mast height and sails were reduced and this ship was constructed without topmasts and topsails. Built as a trading schooner for the Baltic area for shipowner Christian Mortensen, she was also run under the name *Meta Jan* before her purchase in 1963 by British Captain Jim Mackreth. Her name was changed to *Charlotte Rhodes* and with a new rig of full topmasts and a fine set of tan sails she entered her television role.

However, film work and other charters did not earn enough to ensure proper maintenance, which became costly in view of her age. She was sold to Dutch owners who apparently spent more money in decoration and accommodation than on essential structural and planking work. Her chartering plans were severely curtailed when Dutch Board of Trade officials restricted her to inland and protected waters and she was put up for sale again in 1979.

She was still unsold when someone poured petrol in her bilges and set her alight on 12 October 1979. She burnt down to the waterline and was a total loss. In happier days though she paid a visit to Cowes and in a brisk westerly we photographed her in all her glory.

Name of vessel	Charlotte Rhodes
Year launched	1904
Builder	F. Hoffman, Fjelleborn, Fyn, Denmark
Current owner	Charlotte Rhodes Foundation, Holland
Current flag	Holland
Rig	Three-masted topsail schooner
Construction	Wood
Length overall	130 feet
Length of hull	88.4 feet
Beam	21.8 feet
Draught	7.6 feet
Tonnage	99 gross
Photograph date	1971
Photograph location	Cowes, England

CHRISTIAN RADICH

The Norwegians have always been a strong seafaring nation, and when it was necessary to replace the Oslo Schoolship Association's brig *Statsraad Erichsen*, they commissioned a new 676-ton full-rigged ship. With money donated by a benefactor, Mr Christian Radich, the ship was built in Sandefjord in Norway and launched in 1937. In 1938 she sailed to New York for the World Fair, meeting up with the Danish square-rig ship *Danmark*.

Late in 1939, while the *Danmark* remained in America, the *Christian Radich* returned to Norway. While she was under the command of the Norwegian Navy, she was captured in Horten Docks by the Germans who used her as a submarine depot ship. She was taken to Germany in 1943 and in 1945 was found capsized without her masts and fittings, at Flensburg. Virtually nothing but the hull was salvageable yet the Allies towed her back to Norway to her original building yard.

A two-year refit followed and advantage was taken of the six preceding innovative years to improve on her fixtures, fittings and equipment. She emerged in 1947 as a virtually new ship to re-start her training role with Norway's Merchant Marine. In 1956 she featured in the movie *Windjammer* and has more recently appeared in TV's *Onedin Line*. In 1976 she took part in New York's Operation Sail when we photographed her leaving Plymouth, and she continued on to do a tour of the Great Lakes. On her return home she was caught in a bad storm which shredded most of her sails. However the ports she had just visited raised enough funds for a complete new set, a measure of her immense popularity.

In 1978 she set out on a long voyage to the West Indies and the US west and east coasts, returning in the 1980 Boston to Kristiansand Tall Ships Race. She underwent a major refit and accommodation modernization (with bunks replacing hammocks) from which she emerged in 1983. She then crossed the Atlantic for Quebec's Tall Ship Parade in 1984. She has a crew of five officers and eleven men who train eighty-eight cadets on three-monthly cruises.

Name of vessel	Christian Radich
Year launched	1937
Designer	Captain Christian Blom
Builder	Framnaes Mek. Verksted A/S, Sandefjord, Norway
Current owner	Ostlandets Skoleskil, Oslo, Norway
Current flag	Norway
Rig	Three-masted full-rigged ship
Construction	Steel
Length overall	241 feet
Length of hull	205.9 feet
Length waterline	174 feet
Beam	33.5 feet
Draught	15 feet
Tonnage	696 gross; 773 TM
Sail area	14,525 sq. feet
Engines	1 x 650 bhp diesel
Photograph date	1976
Photograph location	Plymouth, England

CIUDAD DE INCA

The *Ciudad de Inca* is the oldest square-rigger still in service today. Her original rig is uncertain but, as she was built in the 1850s for ocean trade wind passages, she was probably square-rigged or at least a topsail schooner. She was made to carry gold bullion from Spain to Cuba returning with tobacco, and her name, meaning The Inca City — i.e., Eldorado — reflects that fact.

She was exceptionally well built, with massive timbers fastened with bronze nails which indicated the value of her cargo. She also has a hidden compartment four feet square running the full width of the ship, which probably points to a smuggling career too!

It is due to this craftsmanship that she is still around today, for she was discovered in 1980 in a very sorry state, tied to the pier in Malaga, Spain, where she had been laid-up for around five years. She had been refitted in the early 1960s and used as a motor coaster along the North African coast but had fallen into a state of disrepair since then. Her owners, who also owned the barque *Marques*, bought her in 1980 for a film project which was ultimately shelved. Nonetheless they completed a major two-year refit in Spain, sailing her to England in 1982. She then took part in the 'Clipper Challenge', a friendly race around Great Britain together with *Marques*, and we photographed her as she left Portsmouth. Her regular crew of eight trained thirty youngsters on each of the various legs of that race and she still takes trainees today.

Her main role is that of a charter vessel and she has appeared in various guises on television and is actively engaged in promotional work. She was in the Caribbean in the winter of 1983-4 and was to have raced from Bermuda to Canada in June. However she had damaged her rudder and could not leave with the fleet.

That night a fierce squall capsized *Marques* and she sank in less than one minute.

Name of vessel	Ciudad de Inca
Year launched	1858
Builder	Built at Ibiza, Spain
Current owner	China Clipper Society
Current flag	Great Britain
Rig	Two-masted brig
Construction	Wood
Length overall	125 feet
Length of hull	88 feet
Beam	25 feet
Draught	10 feet
Tonnage	151 gross; 350 displ.
Sail area	8,952 sq. feet
Engines	2 x 150 bhp Baudoin diesels
Photograph date	1982
Photograph location	Isle of Wight, England

CLUB MÉDITERRANÉE

This bermudan-rigged schooner was built under the sponsorship of Club Méditerranée for the Single-Handed Trans-Atlantic Race of 1976. Her steel hull was built in three sections and welded together before being launched upside down. Three wire strops were then attached to tip her onto an even keel (the keel being some sixty tons of lead). Four masts were erected on deck to a maximum 125 feet high and over 8,000 square feet of sail spread over eight sails were added to make this yacht a truly awesome sight. All the more incredible that one man should be expected to manage a vessel of this magnitude single-handed.

On 5 June 1976, Frenchman Alain Colas steered her through a fleet of 125 competitors in the race from Plymouth to Newport, Rhode Island. Severe gales lashed the fleet and Colas was forced to hove-to in order to repair most of the sails. She could only continue at two-thirds efficiency and failed to take the expected line honours. That one man managed to sail her across is a measure of Colas's skill.

The Club Méditerranée then used her as part of their holiday organization out of Guadeloupe and Martinique in the Caribbean. Her normal cruising speed is around twelve knots, but during a near cyclone she reached twenty-five knots! She is now owned by Bernard Tapie who purchased her in 1983.

She is pictured here at the start of the Trans-Atlantic Race in 1976, threading her way through a mass of spectators. Behind her can be seen Eric Tabarly in *Pen Duick VI*, the eventual winner. Under her new owner she is expected to compete in future sail training events under her new name, *La Vie Claire*.

Name of vessel	Club Méditerranée
Year launched	1976
Designer	M. Bigoin
Builder	Arsenal de Toulon, France
Current owner	Bernard Tapie, France
Current flag	France
Rig	Four-masted bermudan schooner
Construction	Steel
Length overall	236 feet
Length waterline	218 feet
Beam	31.5 feet
Draught	19 feet
Tonnage	300 gross
Sail area	8,300 sq. feet
Engines	1 x 360 bhp Baudoin diesel
Photograph date	1976
Photograph location	Plymouth, England

CROCE DEL SUD

In September 1982, Sardinia held its first 'Classic Yacht Regatta'. The event sponsored by *Nautica* Magazine and Alfa Romeo drew together some twenty vessels, from the small 1893 French yacht, *Felice Manin;* to the largest competitor, *Croce del Sud*, an Italian three-masted schooner. Entrants had to participate in three races, a bridge tournament and a round of golf!

This private yacht was designed and built by Martinolich of Italy and her owner M. Vela uses her for extended cruising in the Mediterranean. She is built of steel and was launched in 1931.

Name of vessel	Croce del Sud
Year launched	1931
Designer	Martinolich
Builder	Martinolich, Lussinpiccolo (Yugoslavia)
Current owner	M. Vela, Italy
Current flag	Italy
Rig	Three-masted schooner
Construction	Steel
Length overall	123.83 feet
Length of hull	114.91 feet
Length waterline	91.44 feet
Beam	23.77 feet
Draught	16.76 feet
Tonnage	174.89 gross
Sail area	4,689.59 sq. feet
Engines	2 x 240 bhp Volvo Penta diesels
Photograph date	1982
Photograph location	Sardinia, Italy

CUTTY SARK

From the mid 1850s until the 1870s, the clippers, 'greyhounds' of the sea, would sail from China to Britain around Africa and the Cape of Good Hope, vying with one another to be the first home with the new crop of tea.

The great clipper *Thermopylae* was considered to be the fastest when Hercules Linton was asked to design a faster ship. She was launched in 1869, the same year that saw the opening of the Suez Canal which sounded the death knell for the China clippers. That route considerably shortened the passage time for the steamers, but the prevailing winds on that route were unsuitable for the sailing ships, who still had to sail the long way around.

The effect was not immediate though and *Cutty Sark* paid her way for eight years, but she never had the opportunity of beating *Thermopylae's* record. She was moved to general cargo duties until 1883 when she came into her own on the wool run between Australia and Great Britain. For ten years she was the fastest boat home, even beating her old rival *Thermopylae*. In 1895 she was sold to Portugal and for the next twenty-seven years worked as a tramp sailer under the name *Maria do Amparo*.

In 1922 the British Captain Wilfred Dowman purchased her for £3,750. She had been changed to a barquentine but he had her re-rigged as a clipper for use as a stationary training ship. On his death in 1936 she was given to the Thames Nautical Training College who in turn donated her to the 'Cutty Sark Preservation Society' in 1949. After an extensive refit, she was opened to the public by Her Majesty the Queen in 1957, at the dry dock overlooking the Thames at Greenwich.

Name of vessel	Cutty Sark
Year launched	1869
Designer	Hercules Linton
Builder	Scott & Linton Ltd and Denny Bros. Dumbarton, Scotland
Current owner	Cutty Sark Preservation Society, Greenwich, England
Current flag	Great Britain
Rig	Three-masted full-rigged ship
Construction	Wood
Length overall	280 feet
Length of hull	224 feet
Length waterline	212.5 feet
Beam	36 feet
Draught	20 feet
Tonnage	963 gross; 2,100 displ.
Sail area	32,800 sq. feet (ten miles of rigging)
Engines	none
Photograph date	1981
Photograph location	Greenwich, England

CYNARA

Cynara is a beautiful and typical example of a luxury yacht of 'between the wars' vintage. Today her varnished joinery and brasswork have been carefully restored and preserved, reflecting the style of the English afloat during that era. It appears that her original owner was V.G. Grace of London and he kept *Cynara* homeported in Copenhagen. In 1934 she was under the ownership of the Marquess of Northampton, who registered her in Gosport, Hampshire.

After a spell in Bermuda and Caribbean waters she was sold to Japanese owners in 1981. She took part in the Osaka World Sail Festival in 1983 and, although still in pristine condition, she is restricted through age to local coastal cruising. In 1976 she visited Cowes (where our picture was taken) for the August regatta and, as she would have attended many a Cowes Week in her past, it was a rather sentimental return.

Name of vessel	Cynara
Year launched	1927
Designer	C.E. Nicholson
Builder	Camper & Nicholson, Gosport, England
Current owner	Seabornia, Japan
Current flag	Japan
Rig	Two-masted gaff ketch
Construction	Wood
Length of hull	95.8 feet
Length waterline	69.5 feet
Beam	18.7 feet
Draught	10.7 feet
Tonnage	73.4 gross
Sail area	3,805 sq. feet
Engines	1 x 125 General Motors diesel
Photograph date	1976
Photograph location	Cowes, England

DANMARK

Following the tragic loss of the five-masted training barque *København* and all its seventy-five souls on board around New Year 1929, and the sale of the four-masted training barque *Viking* later that year, Merchant Navy sail training in Denmark was taken on by the State. They ordered a new ship to be known as the *Danmark*; she was launched in 1932, and commissioned in June 1933.

For six years she carried out her training duties for Denmark until 1939 and the outbreak of war. She was then in America attending the Trade Fair at New York and was ordered not to return to Europe. She was laid-up at Jacksonville, Florida, when, on America entering the war, she was put at the disposal of the US Government. Her Danish captain and crew stayed on and trained over 5,000 cadets for the Coast Guard during that period and at the end of the war she sailed home again to Denmark. The United States Coast Guard were so impressed with the *Danmark's* success that they took over control of the Germany Navy barque *Horst Wessel* which was lying somewhat neglected in a bombed-out dockyard in Bremerhaven. This ship is now known as the *Eagle* and is the flagship of the US Coast Guard.

Danmark originally carried 120 cadets, but after a big refit in 1959 this was reduced to eighty. Her permanent crew consists of nineteen officers and men and she undertakes two cruises per year. The first starts in Italy, thence home via the West Indies and the US east coast. The second cruise takes her to the Canary Islands and on into the Mediterranean. In 1972 she attended the Tall Ship Parade off Kiel, Germany, where we photographed her under full sail.

Name of vessel	Danmark
Year launched	1932
Designer	Aage Larsen
Builder	Nakskov Shipyard, Lolland, Denmark
Current owner	Direktoratet for Søfartsuddannelsen, Copenhagen
Current flag	Denmark
Rig	Three-masted full-rigged ship
Construction	Steel
Length overall	252.7 feet
Length of hull	210.5 feet
Length waterline	198 feet
Beam	32.8 feet
Draught	14.7 feet
Tonnage	790 gross; 845 TM
Sail area	17,610 sq. feet
Engines	1 x 486 bhp diesel
Photograph date	1972
Photograph location	Kiel, Germany

DAR MLODZIEZY

This fine square-rigger is one of the latest to be built to grace the seas. She is also one of the largest three-masted ships at 357 feet overall. Built at the troubled Gdansk shipyard in Poland, she has taken over the duties of the 1909-built *Dar Pomorza* which is now preserved as a museum ship. *Dar Mlodziezy's* keel was laid in 1980 and she was launched in 1981. Fully commissioned on 4 July 1982, her maiden voyage took her to Falmouth in Devon, where we photographed her at the start of the Tall Ships Race to Lisbon in Portugal.

Although owned by the Polish Merchant Navy, she was built from funds raised partly by public donations and her name means 'gift of youth'. Her complement of 194 includes 150 cadets and 44 permanent officers and crew. In 1983 she sailed all the way to Japan to participate in the Osaka Sail Festival. In 1984 she took part in the Tall Ships Race from St Malo in France to Bermuda. In the race from Bermuda to Halifax she lost nine sails in the storm that sank the *Marques*. She later went on to Quebec where she took part in their Parade in June.

Differing from her predecessor the *Dar Pomorza, Dar Mlodziezy* has a squared stern and standing (fixed) yards. She has a continuous upper deck and whereas on the older ship the cadets slept in hammocks in an open 'tween deck, on this ship they have bunks in six twenty-five-berth cabins. In many other respects she is a modern merchant navy ship below decks, possessing the latest maritime equipment for safety at sea.

Name of vessel	Dar Mlodziezy
Year launched	1981
Designer	Zygmunt Choren
Builder	Gdansk Shipyard, Poland
Current owner	Gdynia Merchant Navy School, Poland
Current flag	Poland
Rig	Three-masted full-rigged ship
Construction	Steel
Length overall	357 feet
Length waterline	260 feet
Beam	45.9 feet
Draught	21.7 feet
Tonnage	2,385 gross; 2,791 displ.
Sail area	32,453 sq. feet
Engines	2 x 750 bhp Sulzer diesels
Photograph date	1982
Photograph location	Falmouth, England

DAR POMORZA

Before the First World War, the German Schoolship Association owned three square-rig training ships. The 1901 *Grossherzogin Elisabeth* was taken by the French in 1945 to become the *Duchesse Anne*. The 1914 *Grossherzog Friedrich August* was taken by the British in 1918 and later became the Norwegian *Statsraad Lehmkuhl*. The third ship was the *Prinzess Eitel Friedrich*, built in 1909. She was taken over by the French in 1918 and laid up for the next eleven years under the name *Colbert*.

Plans had been made by the French to use her as a training ship, a role for which she had been purpose-built by the Germans. These plans failed to materialize and even an idea by her later owner, the Baron de Forrest, to convert her into a private yacht came to nothing. In 1929 the Nautical College at Gydnia in Poland were searching for a replacement for the old British-built 1869 barque *Lwow*, which they had been using. The people of Pomerania raised the money to buy the *Colbert* and she was towed to Poland that winter. She was very nearly lost on that voyage but arrived in 1930 to start nine years of sail training as the *Dar Pomorza*.

She managed to weather the Second World War by taking refuge in Sweden and she resumed her duties in 1946. She made her first appearance in International Tall Ship Races in 1972 and was a faithful participant in all class 'A' races until her sad retirement in 1981, when she was handed over to a preservation foundation who keep her afloat as a museum ship at Gdynia. In her time she had won several races and had been awarded the Cutty Sark Trophy for international friendship. Our picture shows her in 1974 — when she took part in a sail-past off Cowes — receiving a Royal salute from HRH The Duke of Edinburgh on board *HMY Britannia*.

Name of vessel	Dar Pomorza
Year launched	1909
Designer	Blohm & Voss
Builder	Blohm & Voss, Hamburg, Germany
Current owner	Museum Ship Dar Pomorza, Gdynia, Poland
Current flag	Poland
Rig	Three-masted full-rigged ship
Construction	Steel
Length overall	310 feet
Length of hull	239 feet
Length waterline	230.3 feet
Beam	41 feet
Draught	19 feet
Tonnage	1,566 gross; 1,784 TM
Sail area	23,727 sq. feet
Engines	1 x 430 bhp Man diesel
Photograph date	1974
Photograph location	Cowes, England

EAGLE

The *Eagle* began life as the *Horst Wessel* built in 1936 by Blohm & Voss. She has two sister-ships, the 1937 *Albert Leo Schlageter* now known as *Sagres II,* and the 1958 *Gorch Fock II.* In the three years of peace that followed the launch of the *Horst Wessel,* she visited several European ports and made voyages to the Caribbean Islands. The outbreak of war found her in the Baltic where she was destined to become a supply ship. She even claims to have brought down three Russian planes with her gunfire. She avoided serious damage and was found at Bremerhaven after the war.

Following the training success with the Danish *Danmark* during the war years, the US Coast Guard, on the advise of *Danmark's* captain, took over the *Horst Wessel.* They re-named her *Eagle* and she is now the flagship of their Coast Guard fleet. Every trainee has to spend some time on her before qualifying and 180 cadets at a time spend up to two and a half months aboard. Nineteen officers and twenty-six crew are permanently stationed on board, and due to the cadets strict academic timetable *Eagle* is usually unable to attend all the Tall Ships gatherings.

She was, though, the host ship for the grand Operation Sail off New York in 1976 when she sported her new Coast Guard stripe and caused considerable comment among purists — but added colour to our picture! In 1984 she took part in the Tall Ship Race from Bermuda to Halifax and reportedly suffered a knockdown, which put her yards in the water and caused her to 'hove to' for a day.

Name of vessel	Eagle
Year launched	1936
Designer	Blohm & Voss
Builder	Blohm & Voss, Hamburg, Germany
Current owner	United States Coastguard Academy, New London, Conn., USA
Current flag	United States of America
Rig	Three-masted barque
Construction	Steel
Length overall	294.4 feet
Length of hull	265.8 feet
Length waterline	230.5 feet
Beam	39.3 feet
Draught	17 feet
Tonnage	1,800 gross; 1,816 displ; 1,561 TM
Sail area	21,345 sq. feet
Engines	1 x 750 bhp Sulzer diesel
Photograph date	1976
Photograph location	Newport, Rhode Island, USA

EENDRACHT

This schooner is operated along the same lines as the two British Sail Training Association schooners, the *Sir Winston Churchill* and the *Malcolm Miller*, in that they are designed to accommodate trainees of both sexes on cruises lasting from seven to fourteen days. Her five permanent crew consist of captain, mate, engineer, boatswain and cook. She also carries a doctor at all times and together they give tuition to thirty-two trainees. These trainees are accommodated in four cabins, thus making it possible to have mixed crews.

The winter cruises are aimed at adult courses and the summer months reserved for youngsters. These summer months are spent in local Dutch and North European waters while, to optimize sailing time and ship use, the winter months are spent in the Mediterranean. Her annual refits are limited to five weeks and most repair work is carried out on site. Her trainees are taken from all walks of life, mainly in Holland, but allocation is made for foreigners too so that a friendly international spirit may be created on board.

In 1976 she made a special trans-Atlantic crossing to join an international Tall Ships parade at New York and she raced from Plymouth, where we took this photograph, to Bermuda and thence on to Newport, Rhode Island. With her Delft-blue hull and sails she makes a most colourful sight.

Name of vessel	Eendracht
Year launched	1974
Designer	W. de Vries Lentsch
Builder	Commenga Co., Amsterdam, Holland
Current owner	Nationale Vereniging 'Het Zeiland Zeeship' Den Haag, Holland
Current flag	Holland
Rig	Two-masted foreyard schooner
Construction	Steel
Length overall	118 feet
Length of hull	105 feet
Beam	26 feet
Draught	10.5 feet
Tonnage	226 TM
Sail area	5,060 sq. feet
Engines	1 x 400 bhp General Motors diesel
Photograph date	1976
Photograph location	Plymouth, England

EENHOORN

This topsail schooner was formerly a steel motorized fishing vessel used in the waters around Ysland until 1978. In that year her new owners, Pieter and Agnes Kaptein, completely refitted her. They removed the superstructure and gave her this fine topsail schooner rig. She now has an extra yard for an upper topsail and she generally cruises the North Sea and English Channel.

Eenhoorn is equipped for the charter trade as well as sail training, accommodating up to sixteen persons in five cabins. She has a permanent crew of four, and operates with the Zeilvaart Enkhinzen Fleet of charter vessels based at Hoorn in Holland. She is seen here beating her way into a stiff north-easterly wind in the Solent, her bowsprit like the horn of a unicorn — which is just what her name means in Dutch.

Name of vessel	Eenhoorn
Year launched	1947
Builder	de Vooruitgang, Gouwsluis, Holland
Current owner	Pieter Kaptein, Hoorn, Holland
Current flag	Holland
Rig	Two-masted topsail schooner
Construction	Steel
Length overall	108.5 feet
Length of hull	83.6 feet
Length waterline	77.93 feet
Beam	19.78 feet
Draught	9.35 feet
Tonnage	97.64 gross; 42.65 net
Sail area	4,519 sq. feet
Engines	1 x 300 bhp 6 cylinder diesel
Photograph date	1983
Photograph location	Cowes, England

ELINOR

This three-masted raffee-topsail schooner was built as a working trader taking general cargoes around the Baltic and as far afield as Newfoundland. Built of oak planking on oak frames, she was still in active working use when her new owners purchased her in 1967. Her rig, which had over the years been reduced, was restored to its original size and her accommodation was arranged so that she could be engaged in sail training or charter work.

For a number of years she took government-sponsored juveniles on cruises, and in 1983 and 1984 she was under charter in Quebec and the Caribbean for the Canadian juvenile delinquent rehabilitation scheme 'Cap Espoir'.

In 1980, while competing in the Tall Ships Race off Karlskrona, she was rammed in her starboard quarter at the dead of night by an unlit Swedish fishing vessel on autopilot. She survived, and after a major overhaul she returned to her normal training and chartering work. Our photograph was taken of her in Quebec when she joined a fleet of Tall Ships celebrating Jaques Cartier's discovery voyage.

Name of vessel	Elinor
Year launched	1906
Builder	Otto Hansen Shipyard, Stubbekøbing, Denmark
Current owner	Sejlskibs K/S Alta, Ballerup, Denmark
Current flag	Denmark
Rig	Three-masted foreyard schooner
Construction	Wood
Length overall	118 feet
Length of hull	82 feet
Beam	19.7 feet
Draught	6.7 feet
Tonnage	71 gross; 120 displ.
Sail area	4,844 sq. feet
Engines	1 x 155 bhp Deutz diesel
Photograph date	1984
Photograph location	Quebec, Canada

ESMERALDA

Following the successful use of their four-masted schooner the *Juan Sebastian de Elcano*, built in 1927, the Spanish Navy ordered another similar vessel to be built and named *Juan d' Austria*. Adapting the design of the earlier vessel, which had proved ideal for their purpose, her keel was laid in 1942. However while still under construction she caught fire and was seriously damaged.

In 1951 the Chilean Government decided to purchase her and work resumed. She was launched in 1952 and commissioned in 1954. One of the main differences from her sister-ship is that she is a barquentine, having a square rig on her foremast instead of a fore-and-aft sail. Also her hull has a very long foc's'le deck and a long poop deck, separated by a short section between the main and mizzen masts; whereas the older vessel has a four-island profile with two side-to-side deck-houses between a shorter foc's'le and poop.

Esmeralda bears the name of an older captured Spanish warship taken in 1818 during their war of independence, and she bears the figurehead of a condor, Chile's national bird. As part of Chile's navy, *Esmeralda* carried four 57 mm guns and has a complement of around 35 officers and crew including 100 cadets. Her home port is Valparaiso and she often engages in very long voyages across the Pacific and to Europe. She has sailed around the world on a number of occasions, and we have shown her in this picture off the New England coast on North America's eastern seaboard in 1976.

Name of vessel	Esmeralda
Year launched	1952
Designer	Camper & Nicholson
Builder	Echevarrieta y Larrinaga, Cadiz, Spain
Current owner	Chilean Navy
Current flag	Chile
Rig	Four-masted barquentine
Construction	Steel
Length overall	370.8 feet
Length of hull	308.5 feet
Length waterline	260 feet
Beam	42.7 feet
Draught	19.7 feet
Tonnage	3,673 displ; 2,276 TM
Sail area	30,937 sq. feet
Engines	1 x 1,500 bhp Burmeister & Wain diesel
Photograph date	1976
Photograph location	Newport, Rhode Island, USA

ESSEX

The *Essex* seen here is a five-eighths scale non-sailing replica of an infamous whaling ship of the 1800s. She forms the centrepiece at the Sealife Park on Oahu island in Hawaii, where surrounded by two million gallons of sea water in a man-made lake, she treats spectators to a magnificent display of trained dolphins and whales. The dramatic tale of the original *Essex* inspired a young whaling seaman, Herman Melville, to write the classic novel *Moby Dick*.

It was while engaged in whaling on 20 November 1819, the *Essex* of Nantucket was attacked and charged twice by a large and ferocious sperm whale. The ship was holed and sunk with twenty men managing to get away in three lifeboats. The attack took place some 1,000 miles south of Hawaii in the South Pacific at latitude 0°40' South by longitude 119° West off the Equadorean coast. One boat was lost with all hands during a storm and it was three months before the other two boats were rescued. Out of twenty men only five survived. It was later established that ten men were lost at sea, and four died of thirst and starvation to be eaten by the remaining crew. Still short of food and water, lots were drawn and one crewman was shot and consumed before the final rescue.

Name of vessel	Essex
Current owner	Sealife Park, Oahu, Hawaii, USA
Current flag	United States of America
Rig	Three-masted barque. Non-sailing replica
Construction	Steel
Length overall	approximately 102 feet
Length of hull	approximately 80 feet
Length waterline	approximately 68 feet
Photograph date	1977
Photograph location	Hawaii

ESTHER LØHSE

This vessel was launched during the Second World War as the auxiliary three-masted trading schooner *Dagmar Larsen* and registered at Aerhus, Denmark. In 1951 she had her first name change when sold to become the *Iris Thy*. Ten years later, after two further owners, she was to become the *Esther Løhse*, still registered and trading from Denmark.

In 1973 she retired from a trading life when she was purchased by the brothers Robin and Tony Davies from Colchester, Essex. They had previously owned the galleases *Nora Av Ven* and *Clausens Minde*. *Esther Løhse* was a rather basic hull, having lost her rig by then, and a full refit was long overdue. She emerged two years later with her present rig (the square topsail added soon after) and was then to appear in a starring role in television's *Onedin Line* series.

Shortly after this picture was taken she was sold to the German Youth Training Association 'Clipper-Deutsches Jugendwerk zur See' and her name altered to *Albatros*. As such, she sails mainly in the Baltic with crews of young men and women. She sails in the company of two other vessels from the same association, the *Seute Deern II*, a ketch, and the three-masted schooner *Amphitrite*.

Name of vessel	Esther Løhse
Year launched	1942
Builder	K.A. Tommerups, Hobro, Denmark
Current owner	Clipper Deutsches Jugendwerk zur See e.V., Germany
Current flag	Federal Republic of Germany
Rig	Three-masted topsail schooner
Construction	Wood
Length overall	125 feet
Length of hull	93 feet
Length waterline	82 feet
Beam	22.5 feet
Draught	10.5 feet
Tonnage	102 gross
Sail area	3,143 sq. feet
Engines	1 x 135 Burmeister & Wain diesel
Photograph date	1978
Photograph location	Cowes, England

ETOILE

Together with her sister-ship the *Belle Poule,* these two topsail schooners train cadets and reserve officers from the Naval College at Brest. Both ships can set four headsails and their deep square topsails have roller-reefing. Their lines and rig have been developed from the early Breton fishing schooners which had been used for Icelandic fishing and coastal trading.

These vessels seldom venture far, limiting their cruises to the north and western seaboards of France, although they will occasionally visit Great Britain, the Baltic and the Mediterranean. When France was invaded, they both escaped to Portsmouth where they joined the Free French Forces. Being the last ships in the French Navy with this honour, they are entitled to fly the French Tricolour Jack with a Lorraine Cross.

Seventeen crew, including a captain and four NCOs, train twenty men. A single lieutenant is the 'commodore' for both ships and he is the commanding officer of *Belle Poule. Etoile* is commanded by a sailing master. Both ships are so identical that the only real difference is in the small name boards and the colour of the masthead pennants. *Belle Poule* has the sail number TS F30 and *Etoile* TS F31.

Name of vessel	Etoile
Year launched	1932
Designer	Chantiers Naval de Normandie
Builder	Chantiers Naval de Normandie, Fecamp, France
Current owner	French Naval College, Lanvéoc-Poulmic, France
Current flag	France
Rig	Two-masted topsail schooner
Construction	Wood
Length overall	123 feet
Length of hull	106.1 feet
Length waterline	83 feet
Beam	24.6 feet
Draught	11.5 feet
Tonnage	227 displ.
Sail area	7,728 sq. feet
Engines	1 x 300 bhp diesel
Photograph date	1981
Photograph location	Fowey, England

EUGENE EUGENEDES

In 1922 Lord Runciman bought the *Sunbeam I* from Lord Brassey and she was used as his private yacht until sold for breaking in 1930. Lord Runciman asked the noted designer G.L. Watson of Glasgow to design a worthy successor. The new vessel the *Sunbeam II* was launched in 1929 and her square topsail and topgallant were added after the initial sea trials.

During the Second World War she was used for patrol duties by the British Government until her sale to the Swedish Abraham Foundation in 1945. She was converted to sail training in 1947 and carried forty cadets on cruises in the North Sea. She was laid up in 1952 for three years until purchased in 1955 by Einar Harrsen's 'Clipper Line' of Malmo, Sweden. Re-named the *Flying Clipper* she was still used as a training ship and over the next ten years trained 300 officers and seamen for the Clipper Line Company. She took part in the International Tall Ships Races of 1956 and 1958 and was the star of the films *Flying Clipper* and *Lord Jim*.

In 1965 she was bought by the Greek Ministry of Mercantile Marine with funds donated by the successors of the Greek shipowner Eugenios Eugenedes, who died in 1954. Thus renamed she still operates as a merchant navy training ship though seldom, if ever, leaving Mediterranean waters. Pictured at anchor off the tiny Greek town of Poros in 1976 she made an impressive sight in the old port in the first light of dawn.

Name of vessel	Eugene Eugenedes
Year launched	1929
Designer	G.L. Watson
Builder	Denny Bros., Dumbarton, Scotland
Current owner	National Mercantile Marine Academy, Piraeus, Greece
Current flag	Greece
Rig	Three-masted topgallant schooner
Construction	Steel
Length overall	217.2 feet
Length of hull	195 feet
Length waterline	150 feet
Beam	30.1 feet
Draught	17.6 feet
Tonnage	634.4 gross; 1,300 displ.
Sail area	14,617 sq. feet
Engines	1 x 400 bhp Polar Atlas diesel
Photograph date	1976
Photograph location	Poros, Greece

FALKEN

The *Falken* and her sister-ship *Gladan* were built for the Swedish Navy as replacements for their full-rigged training ships *Jarramas* and *Najaden*. For these newer ships, schooner fore-and-aft rigs were chosen to enable quicker familiarization for cadets over the more complicated square-rig. The cadets, in their one-month cruises, are therefore able to spend more time on tutorial studies rather than seamanship skills.

Five cruises per year take thirty-eight cadets and fifteen crew to ports around Northern Europe and the Baltic, and both ships are regular contestants in International Tall Ship events. Their spoon bows and stern counters ally these vessels more towards a yacht design rather than a working vessel, but they are none the less sturdy and seaworthy and able to take the North Sea gales. Continuous generators provide electrical power, together with the continual noise, unlike the British schooners *Sir Winston Churchill* and *Malcolm Miller* which prefer an intermittent generator and batteries.

When the Abraham Rydberg Foundation laid-up their schooner *Sunbeam II*, they chartered *Falken* and took twenty-eight cadets on a five-month voyage, visiting Spain, North Africa and several Mediterranean ports before returning to Sweden. We photographed her when she entered the Tall Ships Race from Falmouth to Lisbon in 1982, and *Falken* is pictured here as she beats her way south through the English Channel.

Name of vessel	Falken
Year launched	1947
Designer	Captain Tore Herlin
Builder	Stockholm Naval Dockyard, Sweden
Current owner	Royal Swedish Navy
Current flag	Sweden
Rig	Two-masted foreyard schooner
Construction	Steel
Length overall	128.9 feet
Length of hull	112.5 feet
Length waterline	93 feet
Beam	23.6 feet
Draught	13.8 feet
Tonnage	220 displ; 232 TM
Sail area	7,570 sq. feet
Engines	1 x 128 bhp 6 cylinder Scania Vabis Marine diesel
Photograph date	1982
Photograph location	Falmouth, England

FALLS OF CLYDE

The *Falls of Clyde* is the only remaining four-masted full-rigged ship in the world. Two other unrigged hulks are in existence but have not been restored in any way. She was built at Port Glasgow and launched seven months after her keel laying (May) in December 1878.

She was the first of nine ships that made up the Falls Line, six of which were full-rigged four-masters, and all of which were named after waterfalls in Scotland. The *Falls of Clyde* was credited by her captain, C. Anderson, as 'making no fuss at fifteen knots' and for the next twenty years she sailed under the British flag carrying a multitude of different cargoes.

In 1898 she was sold to the Matson Shipping Line and became the first ship to fly the Hawaiian flag. Her rig was altered to a barque and she plied the west coast of America until 1907, still a fast ship relishing in being pushed hard by her skippers.

In 1907 she was sold to Associated Oil and was converted to a sailing oil tanker, and for the next fourteen years she carried oil and molasses between Gaviotta in California and Honolulu in Hawaii — a journey which took her some two weeks. In 1921 she was sold to the General Petroleum Company, and after her last voyage in 1922 she was converted into a floating stationary oil depot at Ketchikan in Alaska.

In 1958, when there was no further use for her, plans were made to sink the ship in Vancouver harbour to form a breakwater. She was sold to a private buyer who wanted to save her, but his bank foreclosed on him in 1963 and she was put up for sale again. Fortunately she was saved when the people of Hawaii managed, by public donations, to purchase her and she was towed to Honolulu. The Bishop Museum undertook to restore her and fitted her with four new masts, decking and rigging, plus a new figurehead carved by the famous woodcarver Jack Whitehead.

In 1980 the Bishop Museum decided to dispose of the ship due to financial cutbacks. Concerned citizens of Hawaii got together and succeeded in persuading the State of Hawaii to take over the ship and keep her in Honolulu. In 1982 she was somewhat damaged in a hurricane that hit the Islands, but after repairs she was opened once more to the public.

Name of vessel	Falls of Clyde
Year launched	1878
Builder	Russell & Co., Port Glasgow, Scotland
Current owner	State of Hawaii
Current flag	United States of America
Rig	Four-masted full-rigged ship
Construction	Iron
Length overall	323 feet
Length of hull	280 feet
Length waterline	266 feet
Beam	40 feet
Draught	21 feet
Tonnage	1,809 gross; 1,195 displ; 1,748 net
Engines	none
Photograph date	1977
Photograph location	Honolulu, Oahu, Hawaii, USA

FIDDLERS GREEN

This lovely, small gaff schooner was designed in traditional style along the lines of the Boston Pilot Boats. She was launched for Ned Ackerman of Mystic Seaport and she was used by him until 1977 when he sold her to build his new trading schooner *John F. Leavitt* (which was subsequently lost on her maiden voyage).

Vincent and Agnes Besnier, of Paris, fell in love with *Fiddlers Green* when they saw her lines published in 1973 in an American magazine. By 1977 they had saved enough money to build a schooner to the same design and, in writing to her designer Peter Culler, they were informed that *Fiddlers Green* was up for sale. The Besniers flew to the States, bought her, and sailed her back to St Malo in France where *Fiddlers Green* is now homeported. She is used as a private, family yacht but in 1982 she took part, carrying trainees, in the Tall Ships Race from Falmouth to Lisbon and in 1983 she entered the Race from Weymouth to St Malo.

Name of vessel	Fiddlers Green
Year launched	1973
Designer	Peter Culler
Builder	Newbert & Wallace, Thomaston, Maine, USA
Current owner	Vincent Besnier, Paris, France
Current flag	France
Rig	Two-masted gaff schooner
Construction	Wood
Length overall	66 feet
Length of hull	49 feet
Length waterline	45 feet
Beam	13.1 feet
Draught	7.2 feet
Tonnage	18 gross
Sail area	2,450 sq. feet
Engines	1 x 15 bhp Kelvin diesel
Photograph date	1982
Photograph location	Falmouth, England

FREELANCE

This fine gaff-rigged schooner was built as a private yacht on the Clyde in 1907. She was purchased by the British Government for war service in 1939 and had a number of different owners before moving on to the Caribbean for charter work out of English Harbour in Antigua.

In 1976 her owner, Hugh Bailey, became a local hero when he took *Freelance* and fourteen local youngsters to New York for the Grand Parade of Sail. She suffered at the hands of the weather and the pumps only just coped with the big seas that she met heading north. She returned to Antigua to great acclaim and most of the Island's population turned out to greet her.

For a number of years she was a popular charter vessel but in 1978 she was sold to the Canadian British Columbia Government to form their basis for sail training. While on that delivery to Vancouver she ran aground on a reef approaching the Panama Canal. She was gutted by armed looters and pirates who held-up the crew at gunpoint while they stole everything that could be moved or unscrewed. Due mainly to this ransacking, she was unsalvageable and became a total loss.

Our picture shows her in her heyday. A party of charterers are aboard for two weeks of sea and sun in the Caribbean. A passing rain squall lends a stormy black-sky background and a little 'liquid sunshine' to wash down the decks!

Name of vessel	Freelance
Year launched	1907
Builder	Built at Clydebank, Scotland
Current owner	British Columbia Government
Current flag	Canada
Rig	Two-masted gaff schooner
Construction	Wrought iron
Length overall	101 feet
Length of hull	86 feet
Length waterline	65 feet
Beam	19.2 feet
Draught	13.6 feet
Tonnage	81.13 gross
Sail Area	4,000 sq. feet
Engines	2 x 100 Caterpillar diesels
Photograph date	1971
Photograph location	Antigua, West Indies

GAZELA PRIMEIRO

This three-masted topsail schooner was built of pine in 1883 and, though the records of her first seventeen years have disappeared, she did apparently engage in the whaling trade. Converted to a barquentine in 1900, she entered a remarkably long career in the Portuguese Grand Banks cod fishery.

In 1938 she was fitted with her first auxiliary engine and lengthened by thirty-eight feet in order not to lose the valuable space taken up by the installation. By 1969 she was the last commercial square-rigger and one of nine remaining auxiliary Grand Bankers. The following year she was sold to the Philadelphia Maritime Museum and sailed up the Delaware to be exhibited as a museum ship.

In 1973 she was sent to Norfolk, Virginia for a thorough refit with the intention of entering her for the 1976 American Bi-Centennial Tall Ships Race. She joined the fleet in Bermuda for the race to Newport, Rhode Island, but was involved in a collision at the start. Forced to take avoiding action when the *Erawan* put her engines astern to avoid crossing the start line early, *Gazela Primeiro* was boxed in between four other square-riggers and partly dismasted. She was quickly repaired and did make the grand parade off New York a month later.

In 1977 she was laid up due to restrictive legislation governing foreign-built ships working from US ports. With the new Sailing Schools Act which relaxed these regulations, she was once more pressed into service and she was refitted in 1983 to join the Parade of Tall Ships at Quebec in 1984. She is pictured here at Penn's Landing during the celebrations of Philadelphia's Tri-Centennial. In the background can be seen *Gloria*, *Eagle* and the US Cruiser *Olympia*.

Name of vessel	Gazela Primeiro
Year launched	1883
Builder	Built at Cacilhas, Portugal
Current owner	Penn's Landing Corporation, Philadelphia, USA
Current flag	United States of America
Rig	Three-masted barquentine
Construction	Wood
Length overall	177.8 feet
Length of hull	157 feet
Beam	27 feet
Draught	17.5 feet
Tonnage	324 gross
Sail area	8,910 sq. feet
Engines	1 x 180 bhp diesel
Photograph date	1982
Photograph location	Philadelphia, USA

GEFION

This working schooner was launched in 1894 under the name *Amelia* for a Swedish trading company in Raa. Her first change of ownership came in 1899, and she passed into Danish hands in 1902. In 1909 she returned to the Swedish flag and was extensively used in the Baltic and occasionally to Newfoundland over the next thirty-two years. Her first auxiliary engine was fitted in 1920 and in 1930 she suffered a bad fire.

After serious stranding in 1941 she was ultimately sold to Danish owners in 1945. Re-named *Karen Sørenson* she had her rig reduced to a minimum and was used as a motor-galeas. In 1969 her name had already been changed to *Gefion* and she was purchased by the Baltic Schooner Association, a partnership between two Germans, a Swede and a Briton. She was registered in the Cayman Islands and converted to a topsail schooner with six double passenger cabins.

She was back under sail by 1972 and used in the charter trade, and in 1974 took part in the Tall Ships Race to Poland. Following the Tall Ships Race to America in 1976, she was sold to a Dutchman in 1978. He later registered her in Spain and she is currently based at Puerto Rico in the Canary Islands, where she operates daily and six-day cruises. Our photograph shows her under her Cayman Islands registry as she leaves Plymouth en route for Bermuda and New York.

Name of vessel	Gefion
Year launched	1894
Builder	Built at Solvesborg, Sweden
Current owner	Sociedad Espanola de Schooners, Las Palmas, Canaries, Spain
Current flag	Spain
Rig	Two-masted topsail schooner
Construction	Wood
Length overall	120 feet
Length of hull	82 feet
Beam	21 feet
Draught	9.1 feet
Tonnage	92 gross; 189 TM
Sail Area	4,850 sq. feet
Engines	1 x 120 bhp Burmeister & Wain Alpha diesel
Photograph date	1976
Photograph location	Plymouth, England

GEORG STAGE

Replacing the original *Georg Stage*, which is now preserved at Mystic Seaport, Connecticut, under the name *Joseph Conrad*, this attractive full-rigged ship is owned and operated by the 'Georg Stage Foundation' of Copenhagen. This foundation was set up with funds donated in 1882 by a Danish shipowner in memory of his own son who died aged twenty-two years.

The *Georg Stage II* takes sixty cadets on annual seven-month cruises when they are trained by ten officers. The cadets themselves make up the crew, and the first month is spent rigging the ship, getting her ready for the cruise. This familiarizes the new crew with all the intricacies of square-rig sailing. The next portion of the course is day-sailing around the Danish archipelago and anchoring at night. The rest of the course is made up with extended cruises, usually around the North Sea and across to Scotland.

The old-fashioned rig combined with the ship-black painted hull, instead of the usual schoolship white, make her one of the most handsome square riggers today; even though she is, in the word of her past captain 'the smallest of the tallest'. Since 1982 she has accepted girl cadets yet no concessions are made when they are told to climb to the top of the main mast!

We chose to show *Georg Stage* without her sails set so that one can appreciate the complex rigging involved in handling over 9,000 square feet of canvas set by fifteen yardarms on three masts.

Name of vessel	Georg Stage
Year launched	1935
Builder	Frederichshavn Vaerft & Flydedok A/S, Frederickshavn, Denmark
Current owner	Stiftelsen Georg Stages Minde, Copenhagen, Denmark
Current flag	Denmark
Rig	Three-masted full-rigged ship
Construction	Steel
Length overall	170.6 feet
Length of hull	134.5 feet
Length waterline	123.8 feet
Beam	27.8 feet
Draught	13 feet
Tonnage	298 gross
Sail area	9,250 sq. feet
Engines	1 x 122 bhp diesel
Photograph date	1982
Photograph location	Kiel, Germany

GLADAN

The *Gladan* was built in 1947 and is the sister-ship to the *Falken*. Both ships are named after birds ('kite' and 'falcon' respectively in English), and replace two older square-riggers for the Swedish Navy. Both schooners are laid-up in the cold winter months when the opportunity is taken to update them.

In 1969 they replaced their battery-generator system with that of a continuous load generator. This improved the cooking, heating, air-conditioning and refrigeration arrangements though some cadets still have to sleep in hammocks.

The schooners cruise in company and are both regular competitors in International Sail Training Races and events. In 1976 we photographed *Gladan* as she left Plymouth and headed into the English Channel on her way to New York.

Name of vessel	Gladan
Year launched	1946
Designer	Captain Tore Herlin
Builder	Stockholm Naval Dockyard, Sweden
Current owner	Royal Swedish Navy
Current flag	Sweden
Rig	Two-masted foreyard schooner
Construction	Steel
Length overall	128.9 feet
Length of hull	112.5 feet
Length waterline	93 feet
Beam	23.6 feet
Draught	13.8 feet
Tonnage	220 displ; 232 TM
Sail Area	7,570 sq. feet
Engines	1 x 128 bhp 6 cylinder Scania Vabis Marine diesel
Photograph date	1976
Photograph location	Plymouth, England

GLORIA

This barque was purpose-built for the Colombian Navy and carries seventy-five cadets and fifty crew. Her home port is Cartagena and she has the dual role of sail trainer and floating trade exhibit promoting Colombian trade. Her cruises usually extend along the coast of South America and the Caribbean with occasional visits to North America. Launched in 1968, she was the first of four barques to be built at the Spanish ASTACE yard in Bilbao and her lines are based on the classic German barques of the 'twenties and 'thirties.

The three later vessels are the 1976 Ecuadorean *Guayas*, the 1980 Venezuelan *Simon Bolivar* and the 1981 Mexican *Cuauhtemoc*. In 1982 *Gloria* visited Philadelphia to take part in the 300th celebrations of their founding. *Gloria's* crew manned-the-yards, singing in unison patriotic songs, even the 'button-boy' on top of the mainmast some 130 feet above the deck. Our picture shows *Gloria* in the St Lawrence Seaway preparing for the parade of sail off Quebec; all the sails are furled ready to be set at the command of the bosun's whistle.

Name of vessel	Gloria
Year launched	1968
Designer	Colombian Navy
Builder	Astilleros Talleres Celaya S.A., Bilbao, Spain
Current owner	Colombian Navy
Current flag	Colombia
Rig	Three-masted barque
Construction	Steel
Length overall	249.3 feet
Length of hull	211.9 feet
Beam	34.7 feet
Draught	14.7 feet
Tonnage	1,300 gross; 1,097 displ.
Sail area	15,060 sq. feet
Engines	1 x 530 bhp diesel
Photograph date	1984
Photograph location	Quebec, Canada

GOLDEN HINDE

This galleon is a reconstruction of the famous *Golden Hinde* in which Francis Drake circumnavigated the world from 1577 to 1580. Commissioned to be built by the Devon yard of J. Hinks, by the Crowley Maritime Corporation of San Francisco, *Golden Hinde* was launched on 5 April 1973 amid an Elizabethan carnival atmosphere of dancing and feasting.

Based on the lines of a sixteenth-century galleon, she has featured in such films as *Shogun* and *The Buccaneer* as well as various television roles. Run by the company Mid-Ocean Management she is currently used for promotional work and as a floating museum exhibit of Drake's era.

Elm was used for the keel timbers, oak for the half-frame ribs, iroko for the hull planing and pine for decking, with the finest fir for her masts and yards. She sets 4,150 square feet of hand-stitched woven flax using traditional rigging and 'dead-eyes'. Below decks she carries eighteen cannon complete with powder kegs and shot (though when sailing in Indonesian waters she did carry a machine-gun to ward off pirates!). Her accommodation is period too, with reproduction sixteenth-century furniture, carvings, artifacts and early navigational devices. Her mainmast is eighty-eight feet high, her foremast seventy-one feet and her mizzen mast thirty-six-and-a-half feet.

In 1974 she sailed from Plymouth to San Francisco to take part in the celebrations in 1976 which marked the bicentenary of the original Spanish settlement on that site. Drake had sailed past San Francisco Bay in 1579 and had anchored just north of it. In 1979 she continued on her own round the world voyage, calling at Japan and Singapore. After a refit in Hong Kong she sailed through the Indian Ocean, Suez, and the Mediterranean, arriving back at Plymouth in the spring of 1980. Francis Drake would have had over one hundred men on board; today she has a crew of less than twenty.

Name of vessel	Golden Hinde
Year launched	1973
Designer	Loring Christian Norgaard
Builder	J. Hinks, Appledore, Devon, England
Current owner	Crowley Maritime Corporation, San Francisco
Current flag	Great Britain
Rig	Three-masted full-rigged ship
Construction	Wood
Length overall	102 feet
Length waterline	75 feet
Beam	20 feet
Draught	9 feet
Tonnage	172.88 gross; 263 displ.
Sail Area	4,150 sq. feet
Engines	1 x 165 Caterpillar diesel
Photograph date	1974
Photograph location	Cowes, England

GORCH FOCK

Germany, somewhat stung, though un-daunted by the confiscation of their square-rig fleet after successive wars, set about building, in 1958, a new ship for their navy training. The classic plans of earlier vessels by Blohm & Voss were duly updated since the last launched in 1938 (now the *Sagres*) to culminate in *Gorch Fock II*. Germany had lost three ships through accidents in the recent past: the jackass barque *Niobe* capsized in 1932 with the loss of sixty-nine men; and the cargo- and cadet-carrying four-masted barques *Admiral Karpfanger,* missing off Cape Horn with sixty men in 1938; and the *Pamir* in 1957, when she foundered off the Azores with eighty-six men.

It was therefore no surprise when the accent was heavily placed on safety for the new ship, for the German Navy still maintained that a background of sail training was the best form of tuition for their seamen. The first *Gorch Fock* launched in 1932 was destined to be taken over by the Russians in 1945 to become the *Tovarishch,* and is still in active service retaining that name. The present *Gorch Fock* carries 200 cadets on each of two annual cruises. The first usually encompasses the North Sea area while the second of longer duration takes her across the Atlantic to North America and the Caribbean. She has forty-eight officers and a crew of twenty-one men.

Homeported at Kiel, she regularly takes part in Tall Ship events, usually racing with great success. In 1984 she visited Quebec where she joined the parade of sail escorted by a multitude of smaller yachts along the St Lawrence Seaway. She is shown here at a wet and windy gathering off Kiel in 1980. The wind reached Force 8, and many ships had to shorten sail.

Name of vessel	Gorch Fock
Year launched	1958
Designer	Blohm & Voss
Builder	Blohm & Voss, Hamburg, Germany
Current owner	Federal Republic of Germany Navy
Current flag	Germany
Rig	Three-masted barque
Construction	Steel
Length overall	293 feet
Length of hull	266 feet
Beam	39 feet
Draught	15.5 feet
Tonnage	1,870 displ; 1,727 TM
Sail area	21,011 sq. feet
Engines	1 x 800 bhp MAN diesel
Photograph date	1980
Photograph location	Kiel, Germany *(see following pages)*

GRETEL

Built in Finland as a trading schooner, the *Gretel* is now Swedish-owned. She was converted into a three-masted bermudan-rigged schooner between 1968 and 1974 when she was adapted for the holiday charter trade. Spending most of her time in the Caribbean, she did take an extended voyage around the world in 1974-5. She has a sister-ship, the *Gunnel*, a two-masted gaff schooner also used in the charter trade, which fortunately often gives a second lease of life for these ships of character which might otherwise go to the breakers yard.

Gretel carries a crew of five, including a Cordon Bleu chef, and has accommodation for ten passengers in five double cabins. She has equipment for water-sports on board. Our view of her shows her running with the wind off Antigua in company with the American schooner *Voyager* from Mystic, Connecticut.

Name of vessel	Gretel
Year launched	1946
Builder	Einar Gustafson, Borga, Finland
Current owner	Per Hagelin & Partners, Sweden
Current flag	Sweden
Rig	Three-masted bermudan schooner
Construction	Wood
Length overall	90 feet
Length of hull	77.5 feet
Beam	21 feet
Draught	7 feet
Tonnage	160 displ.
Sail Area	2,480 sq. feet
Engines	1 x 120 bhp Albin diesel
Photograph date	1979
Photograph location	Antigua, West Indies

GUAYAS

Built as a sail trainer for the Ecuadorian Navy, the *Guayas* is based at Guayaquil and cruises the South Pacific with some extended voyages to the Atlantic Ocean shores. In 1980 she took part in the Tall Ships Races from Cartagena, Colombia to Norfolk, Virginia, and from Boston to Kristiansand in Norway, winning the American Sail Training Association Cutty Sark Trophy for international friendship. In that year she also visited Kiel, Karlskrona, Frederikshavn and Amsterdam.

She was built at the ASTACE yard in Bilbao, Spain as a larger near-sister-ship to the Colombian Navy's *Gloria* . She has a complement of fifty officers and crew, who train one hundred cadets.

Name of vessel	Guayas
Year launched	1978
Builder	Astelleros y Talleres Celaya, Bilbao, Spain
Current owner	Ecuadorian Navy
Current flag	Ecuador
Rig	Three-masted barque
Construction	Steel
Length overall	257.2 feet
Length of hull	219 feet
Beam	33.7 feet
Draught	15.4 feet
Tonnage	1,300 displ.
Sail area	15,064 sq. feet
Engines	1 x 540 bhp diesel
Photograph date	1980
Photograph location	Kiel, Germany

JESSICA

This stunningly attractive schooner was built as a private yacht for her owner Carlos Perdomo, at a cost believed to be in excess of five million pounds. Her design specified a large, light-weight, fast sailing vessel for extended voyages and world cruising where the aesthetics of sailing yacht design counted far more than cabin space. Above, on, and below decks she is fitted out to a magnificent standard as befits a yacht of this quality. With a crew of twelve she can also cater for eight guests or trainees and her very existence proves that vessels such as *Jessica* can be built and maintained privately today.

Built in Mallorca in 1983, she came to Cowes in 1984 to be rigged at the famous Spencer Rigging Loft and she formed the centrepiece for the Cowes Week Regatta in August that year. Her owner is no stranger to Tall Ship sailing having once owned the schooner *America*. *Jessica* is pictured here on her first sail trials when her new set of 'Ratsey' sails were found to fit her perfectly. Even with such refinements as electric sail hoisting, she carries a wooden, clinker-built skiff with six oars, so at least the crew will have some work to do! With all sails pulling hard on this broad reach, she topped fourteen knots on her trials through the eastern approaches of the Solent.

Name of vessel	Jessica
Year launched	1983
Designer	Arthur Holgate
Builder	Astilleros De Mallorca
Current owner	Senor Carlos Perdomo
Rig	Three-masted topsail schooner
Construction	Steel
Length overall	202 feet
Length of hull	173 feet
Length waterline	137.75 feet
Beam	22.21 feet
Draught	13.76 feet
Tonnage	332.53 gross; 226.12 net; 390 displ.
Sail Area	15,000 sq. feet
Engines	1 x 550 bhp 12v 71 – 12 cyl. turbo charged G.M. diesel
Photograph date	1984
Photograph location	Cowes, England

JOHANNA LUCRETIA

Built in 1945 as a deep-sea fishing trawler, *Johanna Lucretia* was bought out of service in 1954 by Ber Van Meer who converted her to operate as a private charter yacht and sometime sail trainer. Based at Enkhuizen in the Netherlands, she cruises the North Sea and Baltic, taking in Britain, Ireland, Denmark, Sweden and Norway on her travels. She has a permanent crew of three and can carry twelve passengers.

She has appeared in a number of guises in films and television including the role of *Medusa* in the movie *Riddle of the Sands*. She is pictured here off Cowes on one of her visits to the south coast of Britain.

Name of vessel	Johanna Lucretia
Year launched	1945
Builder	Built at Ghent, Belgium
Current Owner	Ber Van Meer, Holland
Current flag	Holland
Rig	Two-masted gaff schooner
Construction	Wood
Length of hull	75.5 feet
Beam	18.4 feet
Draught	8.9 feet
Photograph date	1979
Photograph location	Cowes, England

JOLIE BRISE

This gaff cutter was one of the last designed by the noted designer and builder M. Paumelle, of Le Havre in France. Her role as the Le Havre pilot cutter No.6 was cut short by the First World War and she was later purchased by the Englishman Lt.-Com. E.G. Martin in the early 1920s.

It was during the next ten years that she earned her fine reputation as a fast ocean-racing yacht. In 1925 she entered and won the first Fastnet race from the Solent around the south coast of Ireland. She won again in 1929 and 1930, and she thus became the only three-times winner ever in that grand yachting event's history. During this period she was also under the ownership of the Hon. Bobby Somerset and together with Lt.-Com. Martin they were founder members and later Commodores of the Royal Ocean Racing Club.

In 1932, during the Bermuda race, the American schooner *Adriana* caught fire. The *Jolie Brise* sailed across her stern and managed to rescue all but one of the eleven crew. The last to jump was the helmsman, who disappeared between the two vessels. For his part in the rescue Bobby Somerset was awarded the Blue Water Medal.

In 1945 *Jolie Brise* was purchased by the Portuguese Dr Luis de Guimaraes Lobato. For thirty-two years he lovingly preserved her and was to become the founder of the Portuguese Sail Training Association.

In 1977 *Jolie Brise* was bought by the Exeter Maritime Museum where she is on display throughout the winter months. During the summer she is sailed by Dauntsey's School Sailing Club thus assuring that after seventy years afloat she is still in active service. Since 1978 she has been a regular participant in sail training races and has been as far afield as Poland and Spain. She is shown here during the Cowes Week Regatta of 1975 while still under the Portuguese flag.

Name of vessel	Jolie Brise
Year launched	1913
Designer	M. Paumelle
Builder	M. Paumelle, Le Havre, France
Current owner	Exeter Maritime Museum, England
Current flag	Great Britain
Rig	Gaff cutter
Construction	Wood
Length overall	72 feet
Length of hull	56.1 feet
Length waterline	48 feet
Beam	15.5 feet
Draught	10.5 feet
Tonnage	55 displ; 44 TM
Sail Area	2,200 sq. feet
Engines	1 x 150 bhp Ford diesel
Photograph date	1975
Photograph location	Cowes, England

JUAN SEBASTIAN DE ELCANO

Differing from her younger near-sister-ship the barquentine *Esmeralda*, the *Juan Sebastian de Elcano* is a schooner setting a fore gaff-sail instead of a main square sail. Designed to train officers and cadets of the Spanish Navy, her complement of 332 men includes 89 cadets.

She was built originally with a long poop deck and forecastle and carried a small navigation bridge above a deck-house. This was later extended to the full width of the ship from between her fore and mainmasts; and her main, and main and mizzen. Exhaust from her auxiliary engine is diverted inside her jigger lower mast and being a true naval ship she carries four saluting guns on her poop deck and foc's'le.

She takes her name from the officer who accompanied Magellan on the first global navigation (1519–22) and who assumed command after Magellan's death in the Philippines.

The *Juan Sebastian de Elcano* herself undertook a round the world voyage, leaving in 1928 from Spain via the Cape Verde Islands, South America, Africa, Australia, Fiji, San Francisco, Panama, Cuba, New York and finally across the Atlantic home to Cadiz.

She took part in New York's Operation Sail in 1976 and was to have raced there from Bermuda. At the starting line however, her fore topgallant stay was caught by *Libertad's* bowsprit. Her fore topmast came crashing down and she retired from the race. She made it to New York in time for the parade and we photographed her where even her masts, 164 feet high, were dwarfed by the twin towers of the World Trade Centre.

Name of vessel	Juan Sebastian de Elcano
Year launched	1927
Designer	Camper & Nicholson
Builder	Echevarrieta y Larrinaga, Cadiz, Spain
Current owner	Spanish Navy
Current flag	Spain
Rig	Four-masted topgallant schooner
Construction	Steel
Length overall	370 feet
Length of hull	289.2 feet
Beam	44 feet
Draught	22.7 feet
Tonnage	2,478 gross; 3,750 displ.
Sail area	28.000 sq. feet
Engines	1 x 1,500 bhp Sulzer Bazan diesel
Photograph date	1976
Photograph location	New York, USA

KRONVERK

In 1917 Finland gained its independence from Russia. However, after allying herself with Germany for the invasion of Poland, Russia also attacked Finland and occupied its Eastern Region. When Stalin and Hitler fell out Finland allied herself with Germany with the hope of regaining her lost land. Their combined forces were defeated and, after the capitulation of Germany in 1945, Russia retained her new lands and demanded compensation from Finland.

Finland had nothing to offer in the way of recompense except her timber and shipbuilding skills. Thus it was that over sixty large three-masted 'Baltic traders' were built by Finland for delivery to the USSR between 1947 and 1952. They were used for trading, sail training and oceanographic research.

The barquentine *Kronverk* was one of these sailing under the name *Sirius* as a training ship. She is now preserved as a floating exhibition piece at Leningrad on the River Neva. This photograph was taken in mid-winter when the ice around her was four feet thick and the temperature was minus thirty!

Few of these ships remain today and only two are still under sail; the three-masted 1951 bermudan-rigged schooner *Kodor*, of 339 tons gross, training cadets for the Leningrad Higher Engineering School; and the 1952 *Zarya*, of similar tonnage, which, being built of non-magnetic materials, is used for geomagnetic surveys. In addition, the 1952 barquentine *Vega II*, operated by the Tallin Seaman's School, was laid-up in 1979 and the barquentine *Kihnu John* and schooner *Nadeszda* are in stationary existence in Tallin and Nakhodka respectively.

Name of vessel	Kronverk
Year launched	1948
Builder	Laivateollisuus Yard, Abo, Finland
Current owner	USSR
Current flag	USSR
Rig	Three-masted barquentine
Construction	Wood
Length of hull	144.3 feet
Beam	29.2 feet
Draught	10.8 feet
Tonnage	322 gross
Engines	1 x 4 stroke East German diesel
Photograph date	1976
Photograph location	Leningrad, USSR

KRUZENSHTERN

This imposing ship was the last of the four-masted cargo-cadet carriers to be built. Commissioned for the 'Flying P Line' as one of six replacements for the German Herr P. Laeisz's fleet lost in reparations after the First World War, she was launched as the *Padua* on 24 June 1926 and put into the nitrate trade with South America. Later she was changed to the Australian grain routes though she still carried cadets under tuition. She was known as a fast ship but sadly lost four crewmen on a fateful rounding of Cape Horn in 1930.

After a short idle spell in the early 1930s she was in constant use until the outbreak of the Second World War. She was siezed by the Russians, who found her in Flensburg, and she was converted to a pure training role, taking the name of a noted Russian explorer and hydrographer.

Based at Riga, she has a complement of 236, including 160 cadets in training for the Russian Ministry of Fisheries fleet. She has participated in a number of sail training events since the early 1970s and she is pictured here off Plymouth on her way to the United States. Her crew have quite a reputation for singing Russian folk songs to entertain the visiting crowds when in port.

Name of vessel	Kruzenshtern
Year launched	1926
Designer	J.C. Tecklenborg
Builder	J.C. Tecklenborg, Wesermunde, Germany
Current owner	USSR Fishery Board
Current flag	USSR
Rig	Four-masted barque
Construction	Steel
Length overall	375.5 feet
Length of hull	342 feet
Length waterline	320 feet
Beam	46.1 feet
Draught	22.3 feet
Tonnage	3,545 gross; 5,725 displ; 3,185 TM
Sail area	36,600 sq. feet
Engines	1 x 800 bhp 4 cylinder 2 stroke diesel
Photograph date	1976
Photograph location	Plymouth, England *(see following pages)*

LIBERTAD

Owned and operated by the Argentinian Navy, *Libertad* was purpose-built for the training of officers and cadets. She has a complement of 392 and her midshipmen would have spent four years at the naval college before undertaking the long annual voyage to many different countries before taking their final exams.

Libertad is certainly a large and imposing ship. She is also fleet footed, having crossed between Canada and Ireland in just under seven days at an average speed of eighteen knots. A full-rigged three-master topping 160 feet high, she is pictured here off Rhode Island on her way to New York. She had earlier collided with the *Juan Sebastian de Elcano* at Bermuda bringing down *Juan Sebastian's* fore topmast.

Name of vessel	Libertad
Year launched	1956
Designer	Argentine State Shipyard
Builder	A.F.N.E. Astilleros Navales, Rio Santiago, Argentina
Current owner	Argentinian Navy
Current flag	Argentina
Rig	Three-masted full-rigged ship
Construction	Steel
Length overall	338 feet
Length of hull	301.1 feet
Beam	45 feet
Draught	23 feet
Tonnage	3,720 displ; 2,587 TM
Sail area	28,450 sq. feet
Engines	2 x 1,200 bhp Sulzer diesels
Photograph date	1976
Photograph location	Newport, Rhode Island, USA

LINDØ

The *Lindø* was built as a three-masted fore-and-aft schooner with a cargo capacity of about 160 tons. Fitted with a 55 bhp auxiliary engine she was launched as the *Yngve,* owned by the Swedish Captain Karls Anders Ogard. In 1939 she changed hands and was given the name *Lindø,* which she kept until 1984.

For the following thirty years she changed hands many times though still under the Swedish flag. In 1969 she was sold to the Baltic Schooner Association and was taken to Hobro in Denmark to be converted into a charter vessel along the lines of her associate schooner *Gefion.* In 1974 she was sold to a Canadian, Brian Watson, and she took part in the 1976 Tall Ships Race. She was then sold in 1977 to Captain Greg Birra of the Atlantic Schooner Association of New Jersey.

She sailed to the West Indies for the making of the Peter Benchley movie *The Island* and we photographed her soon after, in 1980, off Antigua. Later in that year she sailed in the Boston to Kristiansand Tall Ships Race and had a complete refit prior to returning to the Caribbean and Eastern United States. In 1983 she was purchased by the Alexandria Seaport Foundation of Virginia and in 1984 she joined the Tall Ships Parade off Quebec, Canada. In that year she had her name changed to *Alexandria* and, registered in Wilmington, is intended for sail training.

Name of vessel	Lindø
Year launched	1929
Builder	Albert Svensson, Bjorkenas, Sweden
Current flag	United States of America
Rig	Three-masted topsail schooner
Construction	Wood
Length overall	125 feet
Length of hull	90.3 feet
Beam	22 feet
Draught	9.2 feet
Tonnage	102 gross; 176 TM
Sail area	5,000 sq. feet approximately
Engines	1 x 185 bhp Mercedes diesel
Photograph date	1980
Photograph location	Antigua, West Indies

LORD JIM

This beautiful schooner was built as the *Meridian* from a design by the famous John Alden in 1936. Thirty-five years later she was already a popular fast-sailing luxury charter yacht operating with the Nicholson fleet out of Antigua. In 1971 she entered the Round Grenada Race and being the first schooner home was awarded the Beken of Cowes Trophy (which was later to disappear, stolen from the Grenada Yacht Club).

Owned and skippered by Jolyon Bierley, she was later sold to an American and she has since been used on world cruises. She makes a fine sight here as she picks up the trade winds and, with a bone between her teeth, shrugs off the waves as she races off St Georges in Grenada.

Name of vessel	Lord Jim
Year launched	1936
Designer	John Alden
Builder	Lawley & Sons, Neponset, Mass., USA
Current owner	Simon Cooper, USA
Current flag	United States of America
Rig	Two-masted gaff schooner
Construction	Wood
Length overall	72 feet
Length waterline	54 feet
Beam	16.5 feet
Draught	10 feet
Sail area	2,790 sq. feet
Engines	1 x 164 General Motors, V6 diesel
Photograph date	1971
Photograph location	Grenada, West Indies

MALCOLM MILLER

Two schooners were built for the British Sail Training Association: the *Sir Winston Churchill* in 1966 (sail number TS K1) and the *Malcolm Miller* in 1967 (sail number TS K2). They are sister-ships and very difficult to tell apart without looking for the sail numbers and the square-topped deck-house doors of the *Miller* and the rounded-top doors of the *Churchill*.

The *Malcolm Miller* is named after the son of Sir James Miller. The young man was killed in a car accident and Sir James, a former Lord Mayor of London and Lord Provost of Edinburgh, donated half the building cost and led the public appeal for the remainder. The *Malcolm Miller* was launched on 5 October 1967 and she has a few minor improvements over the *Churchill*, mainly in accommodation and engine-room layouts.

The British Sail Training Association, which runs these two schooners, was founded in 1955 and the first Tall Ships Race was staged in 1956, from Torbay in Devon, to Lisbon in Portugal. They operate the schooners for nine months of the year usually at full capacity, with either all male or all female young trainees, except for the first and last two cruises of the year when the crews are mixed adults. The schooners each have a permanent crew of seven, with, usually, forty trainees on board. Cruises last for two weeks; the ships work their way around Britain and hope, during each cruise, to call at a foreign port.

Name of vessel	Malcolm Miller
Year launched	1967
Designer	Camper & Nicholson
Builder	John Lewis & Sons, Aberdeen, Scotland
Current owner	Sail Training Association Schooners, UK
Current flag	Great Britain
Rig	Three-masted topsail schooner
Construction	Steel
Length overall	153 feet
Length of hull	134.7 feet
Length waterline	100 feet
Beam	25 feet
Draught	15.5 feet
Tonnage	218.46 gross; 244 displ; 299 TM
Sail area	7,110 sq. feet
Engines	2 x 135 bhp Perkins diesels
Photograph date	1972
Photograph location	Kiel, Germany

MARQUES

Marques was built for the fruit trade between the Canary Islands and Northern Europe and originally had a 'polacca' brigantine rig (a foremast without doublings or crosstree rigging — a single pole).

She was hulked during the Spanish Civil War and the Second World War and suffered severe damage when, during the Civil War, a bomb was placed under her while she was in dry dock. After the war, General Franco forbade the building of wooden ships, but due to the high cost of steel the repair to *Marques* was felt worthwhile. In 1947 she was rebuilt as a motor schooner and carried on trading in the Mediterranean, carrying nuts, olives and wine.

She was found in a sorry state in 1971 and purchased by Robin Cecil-Wright. He restored her over the next five years to her polacca rig, and in partnership with Mark Litchfield she was converted to a barque rig for her role in television's *The Voyage of Charles Darwin* as the *HMS Beagle*. For this she circumnavigated the coast of South America via the Magellan Straits.

She starred in a number of television and movie roles and in 1981 her rig was increased to play the part of the clipper *China Cloud* in a projected film of the novel *Tai Pan*. The *Ciudad de Inca* was also purchased and adapted for this film but the project was ultimately shelved.

The *Marques* was used for training cruises in the Western Mediterranean for a while before taking part in the friendly Clipper Challenge Race around Great Britain in company with *Inca*. In 1983 she underwent a lengthy refit and a Department of Trade inspection before sailing for the Caribbean in the winter, surviving a force eleven storm north of the Canaries.

In 1984 she won the Tall Ships Race from Puerto Rico to Bermuda and on 2 June she set sail on the second leg from Bermuda to Halifax in Canada. We photographed her in the early evening as she headed north in a good breeze with everything set making a splendid sight.

Fourteen hours after the start and seventy-eight miles out, disaster struck. It appears that under shortened sail in a manageable force six wind, she was laid over on her beam ends by a squall coming out of the darkness. Virtually all of the twelve crew on deck were washed overboard, and within one minute *Marques* literally sailed under the water leaving no chance for those below decks. One or two managed to scramble up through the main hatchway and survivors report seeing the lights still burning as she slid under the waves. Sixteen people were trapped below, including the skipper, his wife and their baby son. Eight survivors were picked up four hours later by the Polish three-masted schooner *Zawisza Czarny*, which by chance sailed through floating debris and saw their liferaft which had self-inflated. After a major air and sea search one further person was rescued; the total loss was set at nineteen with only one body recovered.

The *Marques* disaster is the first tragedy to befall Tall Ships races since their inception in 1956 and only the third loss since the Second World War. The other two disasters were the *Pamir*, lost in a hurricane with eighty-six men in 1957; and the American steel brigantine *Albatros*, lost with five lives when hit by a squall off Mexico in 1962.

Name of vessel	Marques
Year launched	1912
Builder	Pueblo Nuevo Del Mare, Valencia, Spain
Current owner	The China Clipper Society, Lenham, Kent, England
Current flag	Great Britain
Rig	Three-masted barque
Construction	Wood
Length overall	120 feet
Length of hull	86 feet
Length waterline	75 feet
Beam	24.7 feet
Draught	11 feet
Tonnage	154 gross; 300 displ.
Sail area	7,349 sq. feet
Engines	2 x 127 bhp Gardner diesels
Photograph date	1984
Photograph location	Bermuda *(see following pages)*

MIRCEA

Built in 1938 as a replacement for the ageing brig *Mircea*, this barque takes her name from Prince Mircea of Romania, who recaptured a coastal province back from the Turks in the fourteenth century.

Mircea is a sister-ship of the 1933 *Gorch Fock* (now the *USSR Tovarishch*); she was launched in September 1938 and commissioned into the Romanian Navy in April the following year. She had an original crew of 140 cadets, 40 crew and 43 officers, who had only a short time afloat before the outbreak of the Second World War in 1939 put a stop to her cruises.

She was taken over for a short time after the war by the Russians, but was soon returned to her original owners to resume her training role. In 1966 she sailed back to her original place of building, the Blohm and Voss yard in Hamburg, for a complete refit. She usually cruises the Black Sea and Mediterranean coasts, being home-based at Constanta.

In 1976 she joined a multitude of other square-riggers in Newport Harbour ready for the Parade of Sail off New York. At that time *Mircea's* complement consisted of 23 officers, 57 crew and 107 cadets. The other ships in this view taken early on a misty New England day are the *Tovarishch*, *Gorch Fock*, and *Dar Pomorza*.

Name of vessel	Mircea
Year launched	1938
Designer	Blohm & Voss
Builder	Blohm & Voss, Hamburg, Germany
Current owner	Romanian Merchant Marine Nautical College
Current flag	Romania
Rig	Three-masted barque
Construction	Steel
Length overall	269.5 feet
Length of hull	242 feet
Length waterline	198.3 feet
Beam	41 feet
Draught	16.5 feet
Tonnage	1,312 gross; 1,760 displ; 1,727 TM
Sail area	18,815 sq. feet
Engines	1 x 1,100 bhp Mak diesel
Photograph date	1976
Photograph location	Newport, Rhode Island, USA

MOSHULU

This imposing four-masted 'Cape Horn' barque was built for G.H.J. Siemers & Co. of Hamburg, for the nitrate trade run from Chile. Such ships were stoutly built and rigged to withstand the rigours of rounding the Horn and it is a credit to their builders that there are a few of them left today.

In 1914, under her original name *Kurt*, she put into Astoria, Oregon for safety when war was declared, but she was taken over by the American Shipping Board Emergency Fleet Corporation for trans-Pacific freight runs under the names of *Dreadnought* and later *Moshulu.*

After the war she was sold to James Tyson of San Francisco in 1922, but she was almost immediately re-sold to Charles Nelson & Co., also of San Francisco. She was incorporated into their timber fleet operating to Australia and Africa until 1928 when in the face of steam power she was laid-up.

In 1935 she was purchased by Captain Gustaf Erikson, of Mariehamn, the last of the big tall-ship fleet-owners. She was used on his Australian grain run until 1940 when she unloaded her last cargo in Norway. She was taken over by the Germans in 1942 who used her as a depot ship at Horten and later at Kirkenes in the far north of Norway.

At the end of the war she was given to the Russians in a capsized, stranded and stripped out condition. They sold her to a Norwegian who intended to convert her into a motor vessel. After having several different owners she was sold to Heinz Schliewen in 1952. This German had already purchased the four-masted barques *Pamir* and *Passat* together with the five-masted schooner *Carl Vinnen*. All were to be re-rigged and put to use as cadet-cargo ships, but only the *Pamir* and *Passat* ever put to sea again under sail.

After a period of use as a grain store in Sweden and Finland, *Moshulu* lay — a disused hulk — in Rotterdam, Holland. There she was bought by Speciality Restaurants Inc. and towed to Philadelphia in 1976. Her rig has been partly restored and she now lies at Penn's Landing in Philadelphia.

Name of vessel	Moshulu
Year launched	1904
Builder	William Hamilton & Co., Port Glasgow, Scotland
Current owner	Speciality Restaurants Inc., Philadelphia, USA
Current flag	United States of America
Rig	Four-masted barque
Construction	Steel
Length overall	393 feet
Length of hull	359.8 feet
Beam	47 feet
Draught	26.5 feet
Tonnage	3,116 gross
Sail area	45,000 sq. feet
Engines	none
Photograph date	1982
Photograph location	Philadelphia, USA

NIPPON MARU

Launched in January 1930, this four-masted barque was purpose-built to train cadets for the Merchant and Imperial Reserve Navy of Japan. She has a sister-ship, the *Kaiwo Maru*, launched in 1931; this ship was preceded by the 1904 four-masted barque *Taisei Maru*, which was sunk by a mine in Kobe harbour in 1945.

All three were built at Kawasaki Shipyard at Kobe but the latter two had diesels instead of steam power. Both *Nippon Maru* and *Kaiwo Maru* have short yards and small sails for their size of hulls and reflect the stature of the average-sized pre-war cadet. The 120 cadets sleep in fifteen eight-berth cabins with bunks instead of hammocks and receive tuition from seventy-six crew. During the war years the ships were de-rigged and used as motor cargo-carriers and after the war they were occupied repatriating Japanese soldiers.

The *Nippon Maru* was eventually restored to her present condition in 1952, with the *Kaiwo Maru* following in 1955. For the past thirty years they have been actively engaged in sail training cruises, mainly in the Pacific, going across to Hawaii and the western American coast.

In 1976 she made a visit to New York, where we photographed her. This might well be the last the Atlantic sees of her as she was retired in 1984. A new and larger *Nippon Maru* was launched in 1984 at the Sumikomo Heavy Industries Shipyard near Tokyo and commissioned in September. A replacement is also planned for the *Kaiwo Maru*.

Name of vessel	Nippon Maru
Year launched	1930
Designer	Kawasaki Shipyard
Builder	Kawasaki Shipyard, Kobe, Japan
Current owner	Japanese Ministry of Transport
Current flag	Japan
Rig	Four-masted barque
Construction	Steel
Length overall	318.4 feet
Length of hull	306.8 feet
Length waterline	256.7 feet
Beam	42.5 feet
Draught	20.2 feet
Tonnage	2,285.77 gross; 4,043 displ.
Sail area	25,800 sq. feet
Engines	2 x 600 bhp diesels
Photograph date	1976
Photograph location	Newport, Rhode Island, USA

NONSUCH

In 1668 the small ketch *Nonsuch* sailed to Canada to open up the direct trade route from Europe to the Hudson Bay. Traders had been using the river system to the St Lawrence for their lucrative fur trade and they wished to avoid the taxes imposed on them along that route. The success of that trip led to the Hudson Bay Company's incorporation in 1670.

The original *Nonsuch* was a typical seventeenth-century ketch, having a tall mainmast and a smaller mizzen, both carrying square sails. It is believed she was built in 1650 by a Mr Page, at Wivenhoe in Essex. Bought by the Royal Navy in 1654, she was captured by the Dutch in 1658 and recaptured in 1659. She was sold in 1667 and purchased by a group of merchants for £290 on 30 March 1668.

She had a keel length of thirty-seven feet, hull length of fifty feet and a beam of fifteen feet, with a tonnage of around forty-five gross. Her regular crew would have been around twelve men. She sailed for Canada on 3 June 1668 arriving forty-four days later. Fifteen months later they were back in England after a very successful trading journey.

To commemorate their tri-centenary, the Hudson Bay Company commissioned the yard of Hinks & Co of Appledore, in Devon, to build a full-size reconstruction. They scoured the south-west of England for the seasoned wood needed, and the design was formulated by a team led by Rodney Smyth who used references from the Hudson Bay Company and plans from the National Maritime Museum. Old skills had to be learnt and new tools had to be made to build her. She was launched on 26 August 1968 and, after visiting a number of North American ports in 1969 and 1970 after her trans-Atlantic crossing, she now resides as a floating museum exhibit at Winnipeg in Manitoba, Canada.

Name of vessel	Nonsuch
Year launched	1968
Designer	Rodney Warrington Smyth
Builder	Alan Hinks Co. Appledore, Devon, England
Current owner	Hudson Bay Company
Current flag	Canada
Rig	Two-masted square-rigged ketch
Construction	Wood
Length overall	74.8 feet
Length of hull	53.5 feet
Beam	15.5 feet
Draught	6.8 feet
Tonnage	65 displ.
Sail area	1,894 sq. feet
Engines	none
Photograph date	1969
Photograph location	Plymouth, England

ORIOLE

Work started on *Oriole* in 1920 in a Toronto shipbuilding yard but she was completed and fitted-out at a Boston yard in 1921. Her original owner, Mr G.H. Gooderham, used her as a private yacht for nearly twenty years, sailing her from the Royal Canadian Yacht Club in Toronto.

After his death in 1940 she was willed to the Navy League of Canada and she was used early in the war to train sea cadets on the Great Lakes. After the war she was transferred to the Royal Canadian Navy in 1949, attached to *HMCS Cornwallis* near Digby, Nova Scotia, where she trained new recruits. In the autumn of 1951 she moved to join *HMCS Stadacona* and continued to train cadets under her original name *Oriole IV*. On 16 June 1950 she officially joined the Canadian Royal Navy and became *HMCS Oriole*. In August 1954 she sailed via the Panama Canal to Esquimalt, British Columbia as tender to *HMCS Venture* as part of the Officer Training Establishment; and in 1963 she was senior ship in the four-boat Auxiliary Training Squadron. In 1978 she became an independent command, still based in British Columbia and spending her time in the North Pacific.

She is now the longest serving ship in the Canadian Navy and is regarded with affection and esteem. She has a complement of eight crew, including two officers, and fourteen junior officers under training, and latterly women have been included as crew members. She cruises the islands around Victoria and Vancouver and she enters the ocean races that take part in her area, namely the Swiftsure, the Maui and the Transpac Race.

Oriole carries no winches for sail handling but relies on muscle power, and rigs all halyards and running backstays 'luff upon luff' to achieve the necessary pull. We photographed her, and her famous 6,600 square feet of spinnaker depicting the oriole bird, off Waikiki beach during the Tall Ships Race from Hawaii to Canada.

Name of vessel	Oriole
Year launched	1921
Designer	Owens Co. New York
Builder	Built at Toronto, completed at Boston
Current owner	Royal Canadian Navy
Current flag	Canada
Rig	Two-masted bermudan ketch
Length overall	102 feet
Beam	19 feet
Draught	9 feet
Tonnage	75 displ.
Sail area	11,000 sq. feet
Photograph date	1977
Photograph location	Hawaii, USA

OUR SVANEN

This traditional wooden barquentine was built as an engineless, three-masted trading schooner, and until her purchase in 1969, she carried malt for the Tuborg brewery in Denmark. Her new owners, Douglas and Margaret Havers, spent the next ten years refitting and converting her into her present barquentine rig. The conversion was completed in Poole, Dorset, and she was registered at Stornoway in Scotland.

In the winter of 1982-3 she underwent another major overhaul at Troense, Denmark, in order to improve her appearance and performance. Her mizzen sail was lowered and her boom and gaff extended, the wheel-house was removed and her wheel positioned aft.

After her initial ten-year refit, she sailed from Britain to Vancouver, via Barbados, Panama and San Francisco. At Vancouver she was given a long-term charter by the Royal Canadian Cadets for training in local and foreign waters. She carries seventeen such cadets trained by her crew of five.

In 1982 she took part in the Tall Ships Race from La Guaira, Venezuela to Southampton, via Philadelphia, Newport and Lisbon. In 1983 she sailed to Florida and Newfoundland returning to winter in Florida and the West Indies. She took part in the 1984 Tall Ships Race from Puerto Rico to Bermuda and then on to Quebec via Halifax. The start of the Bermuda to Halifax race was in the aftermath of exceedingly strong winds (which returned that night with a vengeance) and *Our Svanen* looked truly splendid after her improvements as she headed north on a broad reach.

Name of vessel	Our Svanen
Year launched	1922
Builder	K. Andersen, Frederikssund, Denmark
Current owner	Douglas & Margaret Havers
Current flag	Great Britain
Rig	Three-masted barquentine
Construction	Wood
Length overall	130 feet
Length of hull	90 feet
Beam	23.5 feet
Draught	10 feet
Tonnage	100 gross
Sail area	5,900 sq. feet
Engines	1 x 134 bhp diesel
Photograph date	1984
Photograph location	Bermuda

PALINURO

This steel barquentine started life built for the Grand Banks fishery trade and her home port was St Malo in France. Originally named the *Commandant Louis Richard,* she was one of the last remaining sailing French Grand Bankers in service when she gave up the fishery in 1947. Renamed the *Jean Marc Aline,* she fished in the Southern Indian Ocean for one or two seasons before being sold to the Italian Navy in 1951, where she was commissioned in 1955. Although her short and thick pole masts are original, she has had her poop deck lengthened to accommodate extra cadets.

She now sails in the Mediterranean and is based at La Maddalena in Sardinia. She is run by the School for Warrant Officers and she has a crew of seventeen officers and forty-four men, who train fifty cadets.

Unlike Italy's other training ship, the *Amerigo Vespucci,* she does not participate in the International Tall Ship gatherings but she does attend various local events. In 1982 she hosted the first 'Classic Yacht Regatta' at Porto Cervo in Sardinia, and we picture her here as her cadets make ready for the day's sailing.

Name of vessel	Palinuro
Year launched	1934
Builder	Dubigeon, Nantes, France
Current owner	Italian Navy
Current flag	Italy
Rig	Three-masted barquentine
Construction	Steel
Length overall	226.2 feet
Length of hull	177.2 feet
Beam	33 feet
Draught	15.8 feet
Tonnage	858 gross; 1,341 displ.
Sail area	9,675 sq. feet
Engines	1 x 375 bhp diesel
Photograph date	1982
Photograph location	Sardinia

PAMIR

The *Pamir* was built for the 'Flying-P' line of the German company of F. Laeisz Co. and was engaged in the nitrate trade run until the outbreak of war in 1914. She lay at anchor off the Canary Islands until she was handed over to the Italians in 1919. They could not use her and so they sold her back to F. Laeisz and she resumed her original trade in 1922. The company had once owned fourteen such ships, all seized after the First World War, but they at once proceeded to purchase six back and build another two.

However, by the early thirties, these tall ships were proving uneconomical to run and the company decided to dispose of their older vessels. Captain Gustav Erikson, the well-known Finnish sailing-fleet owner, purchased the *Pamir* for the grain run from Australia to Europe; but upon Finland's entry into the Second World War on the side of Germany, *Pamir* was seized when in New Zealand. Run by the Union Steamship Company she sailed between New Zealand and San Francisco carrying wool out and grain back until 1949 when, un-profitable, she was laid up.

Rejected by the New Zealand Navy as a training ship, she was sold to a Belgian breakers yard and towed to Antwerp for scrapping. However, at the last minute, she and the *Passat* were purchased by two German partners who had the two ships converted into cargo-carrying trainers, but they were laid up in the mid 1950s for financial reasons. *Pamir's* sixth and final owners were a consortium of forty German shipowners, led by the Landesbank of Schleswig Holstein. After she had made five voyages in partnership with the *Passat*, from 1954 to 1957, she was found to be too expensive to run, and it was decided to lay up the two barques upon their final return to Germany.

Returning from Argentina, both ships were hit by hurricane Carrie 600 miles south-west of the Azores. *Passat* only just survived to return to Hamburg. She is now owned by the City of Lubeck and is preserved as a museum ship and youth centre at Travemunde. *Pamir*, however, did not fare so well. As a result of her cargo shifting, she foundered on 21 September 1957 and thirty-four crewmen together with fifty-two cadets were lost.

Name of vessel	Pamir
Year launched	1905
Designer	Blohm & Voss
Builder	Blohm & Voss, Hamburg, Germany
Current owner	Landesbank Schleswig Holstein
Current flag	Germany
Rig	Four-masted barque
Construction	Steel
Length overall	370 feet
Length waterline	316 feet
Beam	46 feet
Draught	26.2 feet
Tonnage	2,798 gross; 3,020 displ.
Engines	1 x 900 bhp Krupp diesel
Photograph date	1955
Photograph location	Cowes, England

PHOENIX

The *Phoenix* was launched in 1929 as the auxiliary fore and aft schooner *Anna*. Built of oak planking on oak frames, she was a typical Baltic trader carrying cargoes across the Baltic and North Sea. She underwent a great number of ownership changes, changing her name as she went. At one time she was a mission ship and at one stage she was altered to carry timber lengthwise through a loading port in her starboard bow.

In 1942 she was re-rigged as a ketch under the name *Palmeto* and further cut-down in 1964. Her last eight years in trade were as the *Gabriel* of Skaelskør.

In 1974 she was purchased by an Anglo-Dutch couple, John and Frederika Charles, and converted to a brigantine in Holland. As the *Phoenix* she was then registered in Ireland. Her maiden voyage under that guise was in the 1976 Tall Ships Race from Plymouth to Bermuda and America to celebrate the United States Bicentennial, and she was under charter to the London-based 'Mariners International'.

In 1979 she was re-registered under the Dutch flag for chartering in local waters and was to be sold in 1979 to two Dutch businessmen. One was arrested the following year on a number of charges; the other disappeared to Spain. *Phoenix* was impounded by the Dutch Inland Revenue and subsequently sold to an English sailmaker, Mr Jack Bethel, in 1981.

She was re-sold the following year to Mr Barry Brenner and under British registry she sailed, after a complete refit allowing accommodation for twenty-six, for Montego Bay, Jamaica, where she operated day cruises for tourists. In 1984 she transferred these operations to Bermuda.

Name of vessel	Phoenix
Year launched	1929
Builder	Hjorne & Jacobson, Frederikshavn, Denmark
Current owner	Mr Barry Brenner, UK
Current flag	Great Britain
Rig	Two-masted brigantine
Construction	Wood
Length overall	111.5 feet
Length of hull	89 feet
Length waterline	84 feet
Beam	22 feet
Draught	8.5 feet
Tonnage	78 gross; 151 TM
Sail area	6,566 sq. feet
Engines	1 x 118 bhp Hundested diesel
Photograph date	1976
Photograph location	Plymouth, England

POGORIA

Pogoria was built especially for sail training and is owned by the Iron Shackle Fraternity of Poland. She is the Flagship of the Polish Yachting Association and trains youngsters along similar lines to the British schooners *Sir Winston Churchill* and *Malcolm Miller*, in that the cadets are not necessarily destined for naval careers. That role was catered for by the now retired *Dar Pomorza* and more recently the *Dar Mlodiezy*. From June until the end of September, *Pogoria* takes thirty-six youngsters on cruises, led by a crew of fifteen.

Outside that period she is chartered, to help her upkeep. In 1980-81 she was chartered by the Polish Academy of Sciences to collect a number of polar scientists from sub-Antarctic islands. She logged over 21,000 miles in a wide variety of climatic conditions and proved herself to be a fast yet safe ship, averaging some 200 miles per day.

In 1983-84 she undertook a nine-month voyage for the 'Class Afloat' programme, with young trainees who were following a regular school year of studies; she sailed from Poland to the Mediterranean, through Suez to Aden, Bombay, the Seychelles, Mozambique, South Africa, St Helena and home. A number of West European paying guests took part in various legs of that voyage, and *Pogoria* has proved that this type of ship can supplement running costs quite successfully in this way.

Pogoria has attended a number of sail training events since her launch in 1980, and she is pictured here off Falmouth on a race to Lisbon in 1982.

Name of vessel	Pogoria
Year launched	1980
Builder	Gdansk Shipyard, Poland
Current owner	Iron Shackle Fraternity, Poland
Current flag	Poland
Rig	Three-masted barquentine
Construction	Steel
Length overall	154.2 feet
Length of hull	131.2 feet
Length waterline	116.5 feet
Beam	26.2 feet
Draught	11.5 feet
Tonnage	342 displ.
Sail area	10,765 sq. feet
Engines	1 x 310 bhp diesel
Photograph date	1982
Photograph location	Falmouth, England

POLYNESIA

Built in 1938 and still fishing, until the late 1970s, the *Polynesia* was the last of the famous Portuguese Grand Banks fishing schooners. She was launched as the *Argus* for the Parceria Geral de Pescarias of Lisbon and, with her crew of seventy-two men, she would sail to the fishing grounds for months on end catching cod from the fifty-three dories she stacked on deck.

These schooners were built to be fast and would often race in international contests for supremacy. She featured in books by Alan Villiers and has graced the pages of the *National Geographic Magazine* in her time.

In 1975, she was purchased by Captain Mike Burke of Windjammer Barefoot Cruises in Miami. She was completely overhauled and her rig altered to trysail with three yards on her foremast. She now has accommodation for 126 passengers with a crew of 45, and she is used for the charter holiday market cruising the Caribbean.

We caught up with her one fine May dawn and her beauty was captured as the sun rose behind her (see front cover).

Name of vessel	Polynesia
Year launched	1939
Builder	De Haahn & Oerlmans, Heusden, Holland
Current owner	Windjammer Barefoot Cruises Ltd., Miami, USA
Current flag	British Virgin Islands
Rig	Four-masted barquentine
Construction	Steel
Length overall	189 feet
Length waterline	170 feet
Beam	35.5 feet
Draught	18 feet
Tonnage	696 gross; 1,400 displ.
Sail area	16,000 sq. feet
Engines	1 x 475 bhp Sulzer diesel
Photograph date	1982
Photograph location	Antigua, West Indies

PROVIDENCE

The *Providence* was built as a replica of a famous cutter captained by John Paul Jones, a noted American Captain. The original ship distinguished herself in action against the British during the American War of Independence and this replica was launched 200 years later in 1976.

Though now made of fibre glass, she does carry real cannons and takes great delight in sounding off a few blanks! She is used for the traditional schooling of seamanship and navigation, and is run by Seaport '76, a non-profit-making foundation. Summer finds her on the New England coast off eastern America and she winters in Florida.

Apart from her hull material, she is not an exact replica as her overall length is somewhat reduced from the original; this is to keep below a certain length, above which she would have had to comply with the more exacting and bureaucratic US Coast Guard regulations.

Name of vessel	Providence
Year launched	1976
Designer	Charles Witholz
Builder	Solna, Rhode Island, USA
Current owner	Seaport '76 Foundation
Current flag	United States of America
Rig	Topsail cutter
Construction	Glass fibre
Length overall	110 feet
Length of hull	66.6 feet
Length waterline	59 feet
Beam	20 feet
Draught	8 feet
Tonnage	151 displ.
Sail area	3,470 sq. feet
Engines	1 x 170 bhp General Motors diesel
Photograph date	1980
Photograph location	Boston, USA

PROVIDENT

The *Provident* was a Brixham fishing trawler built in 1924 to replace a ketch of the same name sunk by the Germans in the First World War in 1917. Built late for her type of design, she had only a short fishing career — she was sold, as were many Brixham trawlers, during the Depression for conversion to a private yacht. For the greater part of her life afloat she has been used as a yacht although she has never lost the hull shape and sail plan of a fishing smack.

One of only four or five surviving Brixham trawlers in Britain, she is owned for preservation by the 'Maritime Trust'. On the basis that keeping her in good sailing order is the best way of preserving and maintaining her, she is on loan to the 'Island Cruising Club' of Salcombe, Devon, who use her as a cruise and training ship.

In 1977 we photographed her during a regatta she sometimes attends: 'the Old Gaffers Race' off Cowes. This event brings together a great many of the gaff-rigged boats of character still sailing in Britain today, and is held annually in the Solent.

Name of vessel	Provident
Year launched	1924
Builder	Sanders & Co., Galmpton, Devon, England
Current owner	Maritime Trust, Island Cruising Club
Current flag	Great Britain
Rig	Gaff ketch
Construction	Wood
Length overall	70.5 feet
Length of hull	63 feet
Length waterline	60 feet
Beam	18 feet
Draught	9.5 feet
Tonnage	39 gross; 78 TM
Sail area	2,100 sq.feet
Engines	1 x 54 bhp Lister diesel
Photograph date	1977
Photograph location	Cowes, England

PURITAN

The schooner *Puritan* is a grand example of one of the luxury yachts of the 'between-the-wars' era. She is now owned by Oscar Schmidt, an Austrian inventor, and she is registered in Jersey. Given a £2 million refit at the Camper & Nicholson yard in Hampshire in 1979, she sailed to Antigua in the West Indies the following year. The passage was somewhat marred when she lost a mast. She has since been used as a private yacht in and around the Caribbean.

Crews on these yachts would certainly have been around forty men, including ancillary staff such as cooks, butlers and stewards, and it is lucky that there are people around today who still believe yachts of this calibre are worth the upkeep. Crews would run today at around twelve, with much of the work being taken over by modern winches and hydraulic power.

Name of vessel	Puritan
Year launched	1926
Builder	Built in the USA
Current owner	Oscar Schmidt, Austria
Current flag	Great Britain
Rig	Two-masted schooner
Construction	Steel
Length overall	103 feet
Photograph date	1979
Photograph location	Cowes, England

RARA AVIS

This bermudan-rig three-masted schooner was built for Mr Hamon, the owner of a large French department store, as his private yacht. She was designed for shallow-water cruising and has a draught of only 4.9 feet with her centreboards up. Her officers enjoy recounting the story of an inquisitive expensive twin-screw cabin cruiser which raced noisily to catch her up. Assuming plenty of depth around a vessel of that size, it ran aground with such force that, as the hull scraped to a stop, the superstructure carried on for some distance to settle a good few feet ahead.

With her three axial centreboards down, fore, aft and rudder, *Rara Avis* draws 13.1 feet and was used by Mr Hamon for cruising for some fifteen years. In 1972 she was given by him to 'Les Amis de Jeudi-Dimanche', the organization which also owns the schooner *Bel Espoir II*.

Registered in Toulon, France, she is used for social work, sail training and holiday charters. Her cruising grounds are the west and south coasts of France in the summer and the West Indies in the winter. In 1983 and 1984 she was chartered by the Canadian social work outfit 'Cap Espoir' for the rehabilitation of 'difficult' youngsters. Her complement consists of eight crew and up to thirty passengers or trainees.

Name of vessel	Rara Avis
Year launched	1957
Designer	Philip Rhodes & Captain Walter
Builder	Built at Terneuzen, Holland. Completed at Groves & Guttridge, Cowes, England
Current owner	Les Amis de Jeudi-Dimanche, Paris, France
Current flag	France
Rig	Three-masted bermudan schooner
Construction	Steel
Length overall	98.4 feet
Length of hull	85.4 feet
Beam	23 feet
Draught	4.9 feet – 13.1 feet
Tonnage	198 gross; 147 displ.
Sail area	5,382 sq. feet
Engines	2 x 220 General Motors diesels
Photograph date	1984
Photograph location	Quebec, Canada

RELLA MAE

The *Rella Mae* was originally the motor vessel *George Washington* and, as such, she cruised the east coast of America for the Wilson Line. Laterly she operated as a ferry-boat between Washington D.C. and Mount Vernon along the Potomac River.

In July 1979 she was bought by R.J. Halcro, owner of the Windjammer Fleet of tall ships. She was rebuilt at Norfolk, Virginia over a period lasting nearly a year. Her appearance was somewhat altered by the addition of four masts plus a rig designed more for decoration than practical sail power!

In June 1980 she sailed from Norfolk, Virginia through the Panama Canal and on to Hawaii, a journey of some 7,000 miles which took five weeks to complete. The *Rella Mae* now takes 1,000 sightseers on daily trips off Waikiki Beach in Honolulu. She dominates the seascape and makes a wonderful sight when silhouetted against Diamond Head or on the horizon as the Pacific sun sets behind her. The *Rella Mae* has been accused of having delusions of grandeur, but if she can give 1,000 people at a time a taste of the sea, is that such a bad thing?

She has a cruising speed of thirteen knots and her twenty sails are set on masts some 131 feet above sea level. Sixty-one crew cater for the needs of her passengers on three decks. The main deck has a shopping arcade and refrigerated and steam-heated tables for the lavish food provided. The promenade deck boasts a ballroom and lounge with the top deck sporting extra lounges, sun-decks and a covered observation area. The whole ship can be chartered, so think about your next birthday party!

Name of vessel	Rella Mae
Year launched	1946
Builder	Lancaster Ironworks, Perryville, Maryland, USA
Current owner	Windjammer Cruises Inc., Hawaii, USA
Current flag	United States of America
Rig	Four-masted staysail barquentine
Construction	Steel
Length overall	292 feet
Length waterline	222 feet
Beam	55 feet
Draught	9.5 feet
Sail area	6,020 sq. feet
Engines	1 x 1,200 bhp Superior VDST diesel
Photograph date	1983
Photograph location	Honolulu, Hawaii, USA

ROBERTSON II

The *Robertson II* was one of the last Canadian fishing schooners to be built. She was launched at Shelburne in Nova Scotia in 1940. Constructed of pine and oak, she originally worked the Grand Banks with twenty men and eight dories. In 1974 she was bought by the Quest Star Society of British Columbia and she was sailed to Victoria in British Columbia to start a second life as a sail trainer. She is operated by SALTS — Sail and Life Training Society — which uses sail training as a means to develop physical and spiritual qualities among its trainees.

Launched originally with two masts and a gaff schooner rig, the *Robertson* at some time in her career gained an extra mast together with a staysail-trysail sailplan. Since 1980, however, in between cruises, she has been undergoing serious restoration and 1982 saw her back with two masts and a sail plan similar to that of the schooner *Bluenose*.

During the summer months she takes up to thirty youngsters on ten-day cruises through the islands and fjords of British Columbia. During spring and autumn she runs day and short cruises in conjunction with church and school groups. We have chosen to show *Robertson II* with her unusual rig as she cruised off Victoria B.C. on the occasion of the Swiftsure Yacht Race of 1980.

Name of vessel	Robertson II
Year launched	1940
Designer	McKay, Nova Scotia
Builder	Built at Shelburne, Nova Scotia
Current owner	Quest Star Society, Canada
Current flag	Canada
Rig	Three-masted staysail schooner
Construction	Wood
Length overall	130 feet
Length of hull	105 feet
Length waterline	86.9 feet
Beam	22 feet
Draught	12 feet
Tonnage	98 displ.
Sail area	5,637 sq. feet
Engines	1 x 250 bhp 611 General Motors diesel
Photograph date	1980
Photograph location	Victoria, B.C., Canada

ROYALIST

Aside from being a most attractive ship, the *Royalist* proved to be a fast and safe vessel whose design has exceeded the expectations of her commissioners. Built for the British Sea Cadet Corps by Groves and Guttridge, of Cowes, to a design by Colin Mudie, she was launched on 12 July 1971 with a naming ceremony carried out on 3 August, by Princess Anne.

She had the honour of winning the Lloyds Register Yacht Award for being the best designed, built and equipped vessel for her purpose, and she has earned the respect of her cadets and officers alike. A dry boat in the roughest of seas, she has regularly exceeded her maximum designed speed of twelve knots and can plough through a force eight with no apparent problems!

Her weekly cruises are usually limited to the south coast of England, but her travels take her around the British Isles, visiting units of the Sea Cadet Corps, as well as trips to the Continent competing in Tall Ship races.

Like her counterparts, the *Sir Winston Churchill* and *Malcolm Miller*, her cadets are not necessarily destined for the Navy but are taught seamanship skills, a healthy respect for the sea, and the comradeship of living and working with others for the benefit of all.

Her rig is designed to keep all her twenty-one cadets busy, though the size of her small square sails are manageable for their fourteen-to-eighteen year age range. The *Royalist* carries four permanent officers with two extra local division volunteer officers. Her home port is Gosport.

With her old-fashioned painted gun-ports, and being the first British registered brig for fifty years, she is most eye-catching and commands attention at all her ports of call. She now has a sister-ship in far off India. Called the *Varuna*, she was launched in 1979 and is run by the Indian Sea Cadet Corps.

Name of vessel	Royalist
Year launched	1971
Designer	Colin Mudie
Builder	Groves & Guttridge, Cowes, England
Current owner	Sea Cadet Corps, UK
Current flag	Great Britain
Rig	Two-masted brig
Construction	Steel
Length overall	97 feet
Length of hull	76.5 feet
Length waterline	63 feet
Beam	19.5 feet
Draught	8.5 feet
Tonnage	83.09 gross; 95 displ; 110 TM
Sail area	4,864 sq. feet
Engines	2 x 115 bhp Perkins diesel
Photograph date	1971
Photograph location	Cowes, England

SAGRES I

In 1896 the well-known Rickmers family of shipbuilders, owners and traders, based in Hamburg, launched their latest steel full-rigged ship, the *Rickmer Rickmers*. They had an established trade link with Eastern countries and the new ship was put into immediate use carrying coal outwards and bamboo and rice on the return trips.

Designed for well-found reliability as opposed to speed, she was equipped with water ballast tanks (as indeed were many ships of her type) together with a tall, powerful rig for long-distance sailing. She had on a number of occasions crossed the Atlantic to North America and to South America on the nitrate run and, in 1905, on losing some yards on her mizzen, was rigged as a barque for economical reasons.

By 1912 she was deemed unprofitable to run due to the advent of steam power. Sold to another German, C. Krabbenhoft, she was renamed the *Max* and sailed to South America carrying nitrates.

In 1916 she was seized in a Portuguese port when Portugal entered the war. Under the Portuguese flag and renamed *Flores* she sailed carrying supplies for the war effort from America. After that war she was laid-up for a short period before being put to good use training cadets for the Portuguese Navy. Her accommodation was increased to house 374 men of whom 200 were trainees. Fitted with twin auxiliary diesels for the first time in 1931, she served that navy for thirty years under the name *Sagres* before being laid up once more in 1962 on the river Tagus, where she served as a stationary supply and depot hulk. She was given the name *Santo Andre* so that her name *Sagres* could be used on the recently aquired barque *Albert Leo Schlageter*.

Twenty years later she was purchased by the German Association 'Windjammer fur Hamburg von 1975' in exchange for a steel yacht. Reverting to her original name, *Rickmer Rickmers*, she has been towed back to Hamburg for a big restoration programme which ends in 1986.

Our photograph was taken in 1956 on the occasion of the first Sail Training Association Race off Torbay to Lisbon (Portugal), when *Sagres* appeared, to represent her country, flying those magnificent red crosses on her sails.

Name of vessel	Sagres I
Year launched	1896
Builder	Rickmers, Bremerhaven, Germany
Current owner	Windjammer fur Hamburg von 1975
Current flag	Federal Republic of Germany
Rig	Barque
Construction	Steel
Length overall	318.2 feet
Length of hull	282.2 feet
Length waterline	259.2 feet
Beam	40 feet
Draught	19.7 feet
Tonnage	1,980 gross; 3,067 displ.
Engines	2 x 350 bhp Krupp diesels
Photograph date	1956
Photograph location	Torbay, England

SAGRES II

Built from a long pedigree of fine sailing ships from the Blohm & Voss yard at Hamburg, the *Albert Leo Schlageter* was to have joined Germany's fleet of training ships but had only a short period of service due to the onset of war in 1939. She did manage two trans-Atlantic trips before being used as a supply ship, only to be badly damaged by a mine in the Baltic.

The Americans took her over in 1945 together with the *Horst Wessel* (later to become the *Eagle*), but they chose to give her to Brazil and she was used by their navy until 1961 under the name *Guanabara*. In that year the Portuguese needed to replace the ageing *Sagres I* and they offered to purchase the *Guanabara*.

After a refit in Rio de Janeiro she was handed over to Portugal on 23 June 1962 to become *Sagres II* and, also carrying the big red crosses on her sails, she regularly enters sail training events. *Sagres II* has a crew of 243 men, including 10 officers, 19 petty officers, 134 ratings and 80 cadets. Regularly visiting ports in the North and South Atlantic, she is shown here off Newport, Rhode Island at the start of the 1982 race to Lisbon.

Name of vessel	Sagres II
Year launched	1937
Designer	Blohm & Voss
Builder	Blohm & Voss, Hamburg, Germany
Current owner	Portuguese Navy
Current flag	Portugal
Rig	Three-masted barque
Construction	Steel
Length overall	293 feet
Length of hull	266.7 feet
Length waterline	230.5 feet
Beam	39.5 feet
Draught	18 feet
Tonnage	1,784 gross; 1,869 displ; 1,784 TM
Sail area	20,830 sq. feet
Engines	1 x 750 bhp diesel
Photograph date	1982
Photograph location	Newport, Rhode Island, USA

SEA CLOUD

This splendid four-masted clipper yacht was built for a wedding present from Edward Hutton to his wife Marjorie. Launched at the Krupp yard in Kiel, she was the largest private sailing yacht of all time. Used for extended cruising for most of the year, she regularly played host to visiting royalty, nobility and all manner of important persons. Launched as the *Hussar*, she cost around $1 million to build, and her lavish interior boasted the finest marble, crystal and gold fittings.

Upon her divorce, Mrs Hutton changed the yacht's name to *Sea Cloud* and she, and her new husband Joseph Davies, sailed her to Leningrad where Mr Davies was to be the American Ambassador. When the yacht arrived in 1935 the Russian Government forbade any Russian to go on board! At the outbreak of the Second World War the *Sea Cloud* was leased to the American Government for $1 per day and cruised under power on anti-submarine patrol duties for the US Coast Guard.

After the war *Sea Cloud* reverted back to her owner, but due to the high running costs, the yacht was sold in the mid 1950s to the Dominican Republic Dictator Rafael Trujillo. He used her as his private yacht and under the name *Angelita*, with the addition of a machine-gun, she became a 'warship' able to avoid harbour dues and achieve various immunities.

In 1961, Trujillo was assassinated and *Angelita* was sold to an American Company who hoped to charter her out under the name *Antarna*. Finding no takers, they laid her up in Panama until 1978 when a syndicate of Germans, led by Captain Paschburg, skipper of the *Ariadne*, bought her and restored her at a cost of over $6 million to her former glory. Under her old name *Sea Cloud*, she now has a crew of fifty catering for up to eighty guests in luxurious style, cruising the Caribbean in winter and Europe in the summer.

Name of vessel	Sea Cloud
Year launched	1932
Builder	F. Krupp, Kiel, Germany
Current owner	Eureka Shipping GmbH, Hamburg, Germany
Current flag	Cayman Islands
Rig	Four-masted barque
Construction	Steel
Length overall	353 feet
Length of hull	316 feet
Length waterline	253.3 feet
Beam	48.9 feet
Draught	16.5 feet
Tonnage	2,469 gross; 4,000 displ.
Sail area	33,950 sq. feet
Engines	4 x 1,500 bhp diesels
Photograph date	1980
Photograph location	Kiel, Germany

SEDOV

The German company of F.A. Vinnen, based in Bremen, had owned twelve fine sailing ships at the start of the First World War. In 1918 his fleet was virtually non-existent mainly due to confiscation and reparation. The firm immediately set about rebuilding its once proud fleet and commissioned a new four-masted ship from the Krupp Shipyard in Kiel. Launched in 1921 as the *Magdalene Vinnen*, she was fitted with an auxiliary engine from new, and the majority of her crew were cadets under tuition from an experienced core of officers and men.

She was engaged in the Chilean nitrate trade until sold in 1936 to the German Lloyds organization. They had for some time been searching for a training ship that could earn her keep carrying cargo, and under the name *Kommodore Johnsen* she was used to ship grain from Australia until 1939 and the outbreak of the Second World War. She was handed to the British in 1949 and they in turn gave her to the Russians who towed her away in 1950.

Under the name *Sedov*, she was put to use as a training ship and oceanographic research vessel used by the Soviet Ministry of Fisheries for the tuition of their cadets. In the 1970s she was laid up but after a four-year refit re-appeared in 1981. She paid her first recent visit to Britain in 1982 when she visited Southampton during the end of the Tall Ships Race from Vigo in Spain.

Sedov is the largest sailing ship in service in the world today; with a crew of seventy training 164 cadets, she can clip along at seventeen knots. Her interior is not as one might imagine, stark and functional; but rather plush with fine wood panelling, and boasting a cinema, swimming-pool, library, lounge, classrooms and workshops.

Name of vessel	Sedov
Year launched	1921
Builder	F. Krupp, Kiel, Germany
Current owner	Ministry of Fisheries, Moscow, USSR
Current flag	USSR
Rig	Four-masted barque
Construction	Steel
Length overall	385.6 feet
Length of hull	357.7 feet
Length waterline	328.8 feet
Beam	48 feet
Draught	27 feet
Tonnage	3,476 gross; 5,300 displ.
Sail area	45,000 sq. feet
Photograph date	1982
Photograph location	Southampton, England

SHENANDOAH

The *Shenandoah* was built at the celebrated Harvey Gamage yard in South Bristol, Maine, along the lines of the US Customs' 'cutter' (schooner) *Joe Lane*, built in 1849. *Shenandoah* was built specifically for the New England charter trade and she operates mainly around Long Island Sound as she is homeported at Vineyard Haven.

She has a crew of eight, including her owner-skipper Robert Douglas, and accommodation for up to thirty-seven passengers. To retain her authenticity, but mostly to avoid stricter Coast Guard regulations, she has no auxiliary engine, relying for the most part upon the winds of the eastern seaboard.

She regularly attends local events for yachts of character and has a fair turn of speed. In 1976 she joined hundreds of other vessels for the American Bi-Centennial celebrations at Newport and New York, and we photographed her as she left Newport on her way to the grand parade on the Hudson.

Name of vessel	Shenandoah
Year launched	1964
Builder	Harvey F. Gamage, South Bristol, Maine, USA
Current owner	Coastwise Packet Co., Vineyard Haven, Mass., USA
Current flag	United States of America
Rig	Two-masted topgallant schooner
Construction	Wood
Length overall	152 feet
Length of hull	108 feet
Length waterline	100 feet
Beam	23 feet
Draught	11 feet
Tonnage	170 displ.
Sail area	7,000 sq. feet
Engines	none
Photograph date	1976
Photograph location	Newport, Rhode Island, USA

SIMON BOLIVAR

This barque is one of the new breed of tall ships to sail the oceans. She was the third of four ships built in Spain for various Latin American navies, following the 1968 *Gloria* for Colombia and the 1976 *Guayas* for Ecuador with her own launch in 1979. *Cuauhtemoc* was the fourth ship being launched for Mexico in 1982. *Simon Bolivar* was ordered by the Venezuelan Navy and her keel was laid down on 6 June 1979. She was launched five months later on 21 November and finally delivered to the Venezuelan Navy on 12 August 1980. She sports a figurehead of national artist Manuel Felipe Rincon, and she has a complement of 294 men, including 17 officers, 24 warrant officers, 51 enlisted men and 102 midshipmen, all destined for naval careers.

In 1982 she sailed to Philadelphia to join their three-hundredth year of founding celebrations, and then on to Newport, Rhode Island where she joined the Tall Ships Race to Lisbon.

We photographed her at the start of the Bermuda to Halifax Tall Ships Race in 1984. She had raced to Bermuda from Puerto Rico and the second leg was started in the aftermath of strong winds the day before. The fleet of class 'A' ships (the big square-riggers) charged across the line at speeds around fifteen knots. That night the winds returned, sinking *Marques* and causing damage among the fleet. *Eagle* and *Dar Mlodziezy*, both big ships, had sails shredded and *Simon Bolivar* reportedly lost eight sails herself.

Name of vessel	Simon Bolivar
Year launched	1979
Designer	Astilleros y Talleres Celaya S.A., Bilbao, Spain
Builder	Astilleros y Talleres Celaya S.A., Bilbao, Spain
Current owner	Venezuelan Navy
Current flag	Venezuela
Rig	Three-masted barque
Construction	Steel
Length overall	270 feet
Length of hull	230 feet
Beam	32 feet
Draught	16 feet
Tonnage	1,300 displ.
Photograph date	1984
Photograph location	Bermuda

SIR WINSTON CHURCHILL

Even with their reputation for first class seamanship, the Royal Navy does not possess a large sail training ship for the instruction of her cadets. Indeed, in the past, Britain has handed to other countries various ships which have come into her possession including the *Dar Pomorza, Sedov,* etc. Whereas full use is made of smaller yachts, there was an obvious need for a large ship to fill that gap.

After the first International Tall Ships Race off Torbay in 1956, the British Sail Training Association decided to work on the idea of a ship of their own to match those of other competing countries. After considerable deliberations, a brand new three-masted schooner was commissioned from the designers Camper & Nicholson. They had already designed such ships as the *Esmeralda,* the *Juan Sebastian de Elcano* and the *Amphitrite* and were not inexperienced in designing ships of this type.

The Richard Dunston Yard in Hessle, Hull was selected to build this fine new ship and the *Sir Winston Churchill* was finally launched on 5 February 1966. Four years of public donations preceded this launch and there was a short delay caused by a freak storm, resulting in the ship toppling off her cradle and damaging her masts.

She was an immediate success and captured the imagination of every British seafarer. Her purpose, during her fortnightly cruises, was to instill confidence and responsibility in the youngsters under her care. Five permanent crew, together with five extra volunteer officers, take charge of thirty-nine cadets of both sexes on cruises in home and foreign waters for eight months of the year. Special cruises are reserved for girls and older enthusiasts, and one of her most notable achievements was her participation with an all girl crew in the Tall Ships Race to New York for Operation Sail 1976.

Her sister-ship, the *Malcolm Miller,* was launched on 5 October 1967. She was named after the son of the then Lord Mayor of London, Sir James Miller, who raised half the initial capital and led the appeal for the remainder. She was built by John Lewis & Sons of Aberdeen and is virtually identical to the *Sir Winston Churchill* except for having square-topped deck-house doors and the sail No.TS/K2 instead of TS/K1.

Name of vessel	Sir Winston Churchill
Year launched	1966
Designer	Camper & Nicholson
Builder	Richard Dunston, Hull, England
Current owner	Sail Training Association Schooners, UK
Current flag	Great Britain
Rig	Three-masted topsail schooner
Construction	Steel
Length overall	153 feet
Length of hull	134.7 feet
Length waterline	100 feet
Beam	25 feet
Draught	15.5 feet
Tonnage	218.46 gross; 244 displ; 299 TM
Sail area	7,110 sq. feet
Engines	2 x 135 bhp Perkins diesels
Photograph date	1976
Photograph location	Plymouth, England

SØREN LARSEN

This wooden brigantine was built as a trading gaff-rigged ketch in 1949 by Søren Larsen for himself. For nearly thirty years she covered the Baltic and Scandinavian coast, sailing as far afield as Iceland and Greenland.

Following a couple of fires in her engine room, she was put up for sale in Denmark and purchased by an Englishman in 1976 with the intention of chartering her out as a passenger carrier in the Galápagos Islands. After yet another fire in 1978 these plans were shelved and she was put up for sale again. She was purchased by Misters A. and R. Davies of 'Squaresail', Colchester, Essex, and they set about a full refit, rigging her in the style of a late nineteenth-century brigantine.

She was chartered in 1978 and 1979 by the BBC for their television production the *Onedin Line*, and has since featured in a number of film and television roles. In 1983 she was chartered by the 'Jubilee Sailing Trust' who specialize in taking disabled persons afloat, and in that year she took part in the Weymouth to St Malo Tall Ships Race, with half her crew consisting of disabled trainees. For her part in that race she was awarded the Cutty Sark Bell Trophy for International Friendship.

The Jubilee Sailing Trust also chartered *Søren Larsen* in 1984 but her deck layout and rig are understandably not geared for disabled persons. They are currently raising funds for the building of their own barque to be named the *Lord Nelson*, and this ship will enable them to take all manner of disabled people to sea.

Søren Larsen is pictured here while attending the 1983 August Cowes Week regatta when she was under charter carrying disabled youngsters on day cruises on the Solent.

Name of vessel	Søren Larsen
Year launched	1949
Builder	Søren Larsen Shipyard, Nykøbing Mors, Denmark
Current owner	Squaresail, Brightlingsea, Essex, England
Current flag	Great Britain
Rig	Two-masted brigantine
Construction	Wood
Length overall	139 feet
Length of hull	105 feet
Length waterline	103 feet
Beam	25.3 feet
Draught	11.9 feet
Tonnage	149 gross
Sail area	5,800 sq. feet
Engines	1 x 240 bhp diesel
Photograph date	1983
Photograph location	Cowes, England

SØRLANDET

This full-rigged ship was built with funds donated by the Norwegian shipowner O.A.T. Skjelbred. He wished interested Norwegian youngsters to be trained in the ways of the sea and he stipulated that the ship would have no auxiliary power.

The *Sørlandet* was launched in 1927 and is run by the 'Sørlandets Seilende Skoleskibs Institution Merchant Navy School. In 1933 she visited the World's Fair in Chicago and at the outbreak of war in 1939 she was handed to the Norwegian Navy, to be used as a reception depot for naval recruits until taken by the Germans at the Horten Naval Base in 1940.

In 1942 she was towed to Kirkenes in Northern Norway where she was used as a detention ship for German personnel. Sadly she suffered a hit from a Russian bomb and, as no repairs were carried out, she was inadvertently allowed later to sink at her moorings with just her masts showing. The Germans raised her and towed her to Kristiansand where they used her as a submarine support ship for off-duty crews. She was de-rigged and a two-storey deck-house was added.

When handed back to Norway after the war, she was in a very poor condition. Stripped down to the bare hull, she was given a complete refit from the keel up. She was back in service in 1948 and resumed her training role of carrying eighty-five cadets. In 1960 she was the last training ship to be without auxiliary power when she was fitted with a 240 bhp diesel.

In 1973 her owners abandoned sail training and *Sørlandet* was put up for sale. She was bought in 1974 by Jan Staubo who, although he had no use for her, did not want to see her leave Norway. In 1977 he sold her to shipowner Kristian Skjelbred-Knudsen, the grandson of the original donator of the funds which enabled her to be built, and he in turn donated her to her home town of Kristiansand. She was given another complete refit from 1978 to 1980 with aid from public donations and voluntary work, and was back in service in July 1980.

Trainees now come from any country and are of both sexes, and in the three months following her re-commissioning she carried 300 enthusiasts from ten countries. In 1981 *Sørlandet* crossed the Atlantic four times in the course of her duties and it is hoped she will continue for some considerable time yet. Our photograph of *Sørlandet* shows her in 1956 when she had the honour of being in the very first Sail Training Race which was held off Torbay, Devon and took the Tall Ships to Portugal.

Name of vessel	Sørlandet
Year launched	1927
Designer	Høivolds Mek. Verksted A/S
Builder	Høivolds Mek. Verksted A/S. Kristiansand, Norway
Current owner	Stiffelsen Fullriggeren 'Sørlandet'
Current flag	Norway
Rig	Three-masted full-rigged ship
Construction	Steel
Length overall	216 feet
Length of hull	185.5 feet
Length waterline	158 feet
Beam	29.1 feet
Draught	14.5 feet
Tonnage	577 gross; 644 TM
Sail area	12,550 sq. feet
Engines	1 x 564 bhp Deutz diesel
Photograph date	1956
Photograph location	Torbay, England

STINA

Built of pitch pine at Sipoo in Finland, *Stina* initially carried sand and coal for a brick factory in Finland. As were many other vessels of her type, she was built on a farm, with timber felled on the spot, by the farmer who was also her owner-skipper.

Stina later entered an era of smuggling spirits and other goods from Poland into Finland, but she made up for this by becoming an inter-island church ship spreading the good word! She eventually passed into the hands of an Englishman who brought her to England, but he was unable to pay for her import duty and maintenance. She was abandoned and she sank at her moorings.

In 1976 she was acquired in that state by Michael Little and, after a thorough overhaul and refit, *Stina* is now back to her old self. Now used for private charters and promotional work, *Stina* has appeared in a number of films and in 1981 and 1982 she was under charter to Mariners International, a non-profit-making traditional sailing association.

Stina has berths for ten trainees or passengers plus a crew of four, and we have pictured her here in a gentle breeze as her charterers enjoy a cruise in the Solent.

Name of vessel	Stina
Year launched	1946
Builder	Built at Sipoo, Finland
Current owner	M.J. Little (Marine Engineers) Ltd
Current flag	Great Britain
Rig	Two-masted gaff-rigged schooner
Construction	Wood
Length overall	107 feet
Length of hull	75 feet
Length waterline	65 feet
Beam	22 feet
Draught	6.5 feet
Tonnage	79.52 gross; 108 TM
Engines	1 x 100 bhp Gardner diesel
Photograph date	1984
Photograph location	Cowes, England

SVANEN AV STOCKHOLM

The *Svanen Av Stockholm* was built as a small inshore passenger steamer, then called *Svanen* and later re-named *Uman;* and she remained in this trade until the mid-1960s.

In 1978 she underwent a major refit and conversion into a sailing vessel with a staysail schooner rig and bermudan mainsail. She sailed for a year under the name *Ghost* before changing to *Svanen Av Stockholm* in 1979 when she sailed for the West Indies.

After a year in the charter trade, she returned in 1980 to the Baltic for the Tall Ships Race of that year. She took a crew of 'problem' children in that race, perhaps giving them a new interest and a chance to mend their ways. She later returned to the Caribbean to earn her keep on short six-berth cruises around the exotic islands.

Name of vessel	Svanen av Stockholm
Year launched	1906
Builder	Built at Harnosand, Sweden
Current owner	Carl Magnus Ring, Stockholm, Sweden
Current flag	Sweden
Rig	Two-masted bermudan staysail schooner
Construction	Iron
Length overall	95 feet
Length of hull	73.6 feet
Length waterline	70 feet
Beam	14.4 feet
Draught	5 feet – 12 feet
Tonnage	58 gross; 61 TM
Photograph date	1979
Photograph location	Antigua, West Indies

TAITU

This luxuriously appointed schooner was launched in 1941 and extensively refitted in 1961 to a quite magnificent standard. She carries thirteen crew and staff and has accommodation for up to eleven guests (among whom have been Princess Margaret and the Aga Khan) in sumptuous cabins.

She has a top speed of around twelve knots, but in our picture she awaits that elusive breeze as she leaves Porto Cervo harbour in Sardinia. She was attending the first Classic Yacht Regatta there organized by the Italian yachting magazine *Nautica* and sponsored by Alfa Romeo. She was not the oldest yacht to attend, however; that honour went to the 1893 French fishing smack *Felice Manin*.

Name of vessel	Taitu
Year launched	1941
Designer	A. Boretti
Builder	Built in Italy
Current owner	A. Matacena, Italy
Current flag	Italy
Rig	Three-masted staysail-trysail schooner
Construction	Wood
Beam	33 feet
Sail area	6,415 sq. feet
Photograph date	1982
Photograph location	Sardinia, Italy

TE QUEST

This trysail schooner was owned and run by the Flint School of Sarasota, Florida and carried fifty-five students. She and her associated ship *Te Vega* acted as a floating campus as well as training ships, and youngsters from America were taken aboard for cruises — usually in the Mediterranean — while still studying on a normal basis.

Te Quest was launched as the *Black Douglas,* and was a private yacht for Mr Robert Roebling, who sailed her round Cape Horn. She later became a fisheries research vessel before the Second World War when she was operated, minus her rig, by the US Navy as an anti-submarine patrol ship.

In 1972 she was purchased by the Flint School who, after ten years' service, sold her in 1982 to a private owner who had her completely overhauled at Abeking & Rasmussen in Germany. Her hull plating was renewed and luxury accommodation added below. She now has a crew of seven, with seven state rooms for fourteen guests. Under her new white livery, and re-named *Aquarius,* she set sail for the Caribbean and the United States in 1983.

Name of vessel	Te Quest
Year launched	1930
Designer	Henry Gielow
Builder	Bath Ironworks, Maine, USA
Rig	Three-masted schooner
Construction	Steel
Length overall	175 feet
Length of hull	157.6 feet
Beam	31.8 feet
Draught	11.8 feet
Tonnage	371 gross; 500 displ.
Sail area	11,400 sq. feet
Engines	2 x 370 bhp diesels
Photograph date	1981
Photograph location	Monte Carlo

TE VEGA

This steel-gaff topsail schooner was launched as the private yacht *Etak* for an American, Walter G. Ladd. During the Second World War she was operated by the US Navy on anti-submarine duties and soon after appeared in the film *South Seas Adventure*.

From 1958 to 1962 she was used by the Stanford University of California as a research vessel and in 1972 she was purchased by the Flint School of Sarasota, Florida. She sailed in company with the *Te Quest* as a floating school, teaching junior and high school students a full American curriculum while giving them a thorough nautical training. *Te Vega* has accommodation for fifty-two youngsters in thirteen cabins, plus self-contained quarters for the master and staff.

In 1982 *Te Vega* was sold in Copenhagen to the Landmark School of Pride's Crossing, Massachusetts. She became a school-ship for dyslexic children and, after a refit in a Swedish yard in 1982, she sailed to the Mediterranean to take up her new duties.

Name of vessel	Te Vega
Year launched	1930
Designer	Cox & Stevens
Builder	F. Krupp, Germaniawerft, Kiel, Germany
Current owner	Landmark School, Prides Crossing, Mass., USA
Rig	Two-masted gaff-rigged schooner
Construction	Steel
Length overall	155.7 feet
Length of hull	135.6 feet
Beam	27.9 feet
Draught	17.1 feet
Tonnage	243 gross; 400 displ.
Sail area	10,400 sq. feet
Engines	1 x 225 bhp Mirrless diesel
Photograph date	1981
Photograph location	Monte Carlo

TERMINIST

The *Terminist* was the last Brixham trawler ketch to be built inside the breakwater at Brixham, hence her unusual name. The next trawler to be built by R.J. Jackman was constructed outside the breakwater and was named *Precedent*. The *Terminist* was built for Thomas Jackman, one of the brothers who owned the yard where she was built, and predictably great care and the best available materials were used in her construction.

During the First World War she took part in what the local fishermen called the 'Battle of the Scruff', on 30 September 1915, when a German submarine surfaced among the Brixham trawler fleet fishing in the Channel. Some of the ships were sunk by machine-gun fire and others were damaged. The *Terminist* escaped but soon came back to the scene to pick up survivors from the Brixham ketch *Diligence*, which had been raked by gunfire, and to tow back the *Diligence* herself.

The *Diligence* was also to survive the demise of fishing sail and later became an inter-island sailing cargo vessel in the West Indies. Still trading, she sank off the Grenadines in 1980.

The *Terminist* remained engaged in fishing until 1936 when she was sold for conversion to a private yacht. She went through several owners until she was bought in 1968 by Lt. John Dines and his wife Marion. At that time the ship had been laid up a few years at Bucklers Hard, Hampshire, the last couple of which she was resting on the mud, with the tide flowing in and out of her. The Dines's overhauled her and put her back in sailing condition, as the photograph shows.

They sold her in late 1972, and she was converted into a floating licensed club at Southampton. Ultimately she was beached on the Hamble River, Hampshire, where she still lies, somewhat abandoned.

Name of vessel	Terminist
Year launched	1912
Designer	R.J. Jackman
Builder	R.J. Jackman, Brixham, Devon, England
Current owner	Robin Knox-Johnson
Current flag	Great Britain
Rig	Gaff ketch
Construction	Wood
Length overall	115 feet
Length of hull	80 feet
Length waterline	68 feet
Beam	18.7 feet
Draught	9.5 feet
Tonnage	40.75 gross; 92 TM
Sail area	2,500 sq. feet
Engines	1 x 38 bhp Gardner 4 cylinder diesel
Photograph date	1970
Photograph location	Cowes, England

TOVARISHCH

This barque was launched as the German Navy schoolship *Gorch Fock* in 1933 and she was the first of a series of six near sister-ships built by the Blohm & Voss Shipyard at Hamburg. Her closest sister-ship is the *Mircea*, launched in 1938 for the Romanian Navy, and her four larger sisters were the 1936 *Horst Wessel* (now *Eagle*); the 1937 *Albert Leo Schlageter* (now *Sagres II*); the 1958 *Gorch Fock II*; and the *Herbert Norkus*, launched in 1939 for the German Navy but never completed. She was used by the Allies after the war for munitions dumping and was scuttled with her last load.

It is interesting to note that the masts of all these ships were limited in height to enable them to pass unhindered under the bridges of the then Kaiser Wilhelm (now Kiel) Canal.

Gorch Fock I was built largely from funds raised by public donations after the sad loss of the barque *Niobe* in 1932, and she was designed to carry 240 persons of which 108 were cadets. Sunk off Stralsund in 1945, she was raised by the Russians in 1948. After a thorough refit she was re-commissioned in 1951 in order to train seamen for Soviet shipping — both the Merchant Service and for the Navy.

She is the second ship to carry the name *Tovarishch*; the first being the former British four-masted barque *Lauriston*. *Tovarishch II* now carries forty-six crew, and trains 130 cadets under the jurisdiction of the Kerson Naval School on the Black Sea.

In 1974 and 1976 she took part in the International Sail Training Races, though from 1977 she was limited, due to her ageing condition, to local coastal cruising and is due to be replaced by a *Dar Mlodziezy* class ship.

Name of vessel	Tovarishch
Year launched	1933
Designer	Blohm & Voss
Builder	Blohm & Voss, Hamburg, Germany
Current owner	USSR Ministry of Shipping
Current flag	USSR
Rig	Three-masted barque
Construction	Steel
Length overall	269.5 feet
Length of hull	241.8 feet
Length waterline	230.5 feet
Beam	39.2 feet
Draught	17 feet
Tonnage	1,604 displ; 1,727 TM
Sail area	18,400 sq. feet
Engines	1 x 220 bhp 4 stroke diesel
Photograph date	1976
Photograph location	Plymouth, England

UNICORN

This ship was built as the *Lyra* in the traditional Finnish fashion, by her owner, Helge Johansson, on a beach near a convenient supply of timber. Rigged as a schooner for local trading, she carried timber, sand and other building materials for the rebuilding of Finnish towns laid waste by the ravages of war.

She was used by her first owner for twenty-three years until 1971, by which time she had been cut down to a motorized sand-barge. She was purchased by a Franco-American, Jacques Thirly, who renamed her *Unicorn* and converted her back to sail, rigged as a brig. She sailed for the West Indies via the south coast of England, where we photographed her off Cowes, to be ultimately bought by William Wycoff, an American interested in sail training.

She was extensively rebuilt in the United States in 1975 and 1976; but following Mr Wycoff's untimely death in 1976 she passed into the hands of several successive under-financed sail training organizations. In 1980 she was purchased by hotel owner Robert Elliot and she is now engaged in taking forty to fifty passengers on day trips on the Caribbean island of St Lucia.

Unicorn has reached fame by appearing in a number of film and television roles, among them as the slave ship in *Roots*.

Name of vessel	Unicorn
Year launched	1948
Designer	Helge Johansson
Builder	Helge Johansson, Sipoo, Finland
Current owner	Robert Elliot, St Lucia, West Indies
Current flag	Great Britain
Rig	Two-masted brig
Construction	Wood
Length overall	148 feet
Length of hull	94 feet
Length waterline	82 feet
Beam	24 feet
Draught	9 feet
Tonnage	190 TM
Engines	1 x 500 hp diesel
Photograph date	1973
Photograph location	Cowes, England

H.M.S. VICTORY

Famous as Admiral Lord Nelson's flagship in the battle of Trafalgar (1805), *HMS Victory* is the only example of a 'first rate ship-of-the-line' today. Her keel was laid down at Chatham in July 1759, during the Seven Years War, and she was launched in May 1765, to be held in the reserve fleet until her full commission into the Royal Navy in 1778.

France had sided with the Americans after the revolution in 1776 and *HMS Victory* was to be used as flagship by Admirals Hardy, Geary, Hyde Parker, Kempenfelt and Lord Howe. Before being paid off in 1783, she saw action in the battle of Ushant (1778), and the relief of Gibraltar and the battle of Cape Spartel (1782).

In 1793 Britain joined the First Coalition against revolutionary France and *HMS Victory* was re-commissioned as the flagship for Admiral Lord Hood. She took part in the brief occupation of Toulon (1793) and the siege of Calvi, Corsica (1794); and after a quick refit she sailed as the flagship for Admiral Man, taking part in the Battle of Cape Hyeres (1795). In 1795-97 she flew the flag of Admiral Sir John Jervis and took part in the battle of Cape St Vincent (1797). She then returned to Chatham where she spent two years as a hospital ship for the floating prisons.

An ageing thirty-six years old, she received a thorough rebuild and modernization from 1801 to 1803 and returned to the Mediterranean as the flagship of Admiral Lord Nelson. She took part in the eighteen-month blockade of Toulon and pursued Admiral Villeneuve's fleet across the Atlantic to the West Indies. In 1805 she joined the British fleet blockading Cadiz. A combined French and Spanish fleet sailed and was engaged by the British on 21 October 1805 off Cape Trafalgar. The French and Spanish fleet suffered a crushing defeat, but Nelson was mortally wounded by a musket-ball fired from the French *Redoubtable*. *Victory* herself was badly damaged and was sent for a long refit at Chatham and was then used from 1808 to 1812 by Admiral Saumarez for most of the time. Her last engagements were in the evacuation of Corunna and in the Baltic Campaign.

Pensioned off as far as a fighting ship goes, she has remained commissioned as the stationary flagship of the Portsmouth Command since 1824 apart from a short period from 1869 to 1889, and since 1922 she has been preserved in the dry dock at Portsmouth. She is restored to her 1805 appearance, when she was armed with 104 guns and would have been manned by 850 men, officers and marines.

Name of vessel	H.M.S. Victory
Year launched	1765
Designer	Thomas Slade
Builder	Chatham Royal Naval Dockyard, England
Current owner	British Royal Navy, Portsmouth, England
Current flag	Great Britain
Rig	Three-masted full-rigged ship
Construction	Wood
Length overall	328 feet
Length of hull	226.3 feet
Length waterline	194.5 feet
Beam	52 feet
Draught	19.7 feet
Tonnage	4,000 displ.
Sail area	42,666 sq. feet (including spares)
Engines	none
Photograph date	1981 (21 October, Trafalgar Day)
Photograph location	Portsmouth, England

VOYAGER

The *Voyager* was built for the head-berth charter trade under US Coast Guard passenger-carrying vessel rules. She is built in the style of late nineteenth-century coastal packets with a very simple and easily handled schooner rig, with only three sails: jib, main and mizzen. She has ten double cabins for passengers.

From early June to early October she offers one-, two- and three-week cruises out of Mystic, Connecticut, which call at places such as Essex, Greenport, Sag Harbour, Block Island and Newport. During the harsh New England winter, from December through May, she operates six-day cruises in the Virgin Islands.

Name of vessel	Voyager
Year launched	1978
Builder	Built at Burgess, Virginia, USA
Current owner	American Schooner Line Inc., Mystic, Conn., USA
Current flag	United States of America
Rig	Two-masted schooner
Construction	Plywood
Length overall	approximately 85 feet
Length of hull	65 feet
Beam	21 feet
Draught	9.2 feet
Tonnage	62 gross
Sail area	2,200 sq. feet
Photograph date	1979
Photograph location	Antigua, West Indies

YANKEE CLIPPER

This attractive staysail schooner was built at the Krupp Shipyard in Germany for Herr Friedrich Krupp as his private yacht. Launched in 1927 as the *Cressida,* she was taken as a war prize by the Americans after the Second World War. She was acquired by the Vanderbilt Estate and was put to good use logging many thousands of miles as a scientific research vessel before her sale in 1962.

Her new owners, the Mike Burke-owned Windjammer Barefoot Cruises Inc. of Florida, converted her to accommodate seventy passengers for holiday cruises in the Caribbean. Twenty-three crew run the ship on six-day trips which start and end in Martinique and visit either the Grenadines (Mayreau, Marigot Bay, Mustique and Palm Island); or St Lucia, St Vincent, Petit St Vincent and Bequia.

Name of vessel	Yankee Clipper
Year launched	1927
Builder	F. Krupp, Germaniawerft, Kiel, Germany
Current owner	Windjammer Barefoot Cruises, Miami, USA
Current flag	British Virgin Islands
Rig	Two-masted staysail schooner
Construction	Steel
Length overall	197 feet
Length waterline	172 feet
Beam	30 feet
Draught	17 feet
Tonnage	350 gross; 600 displ.
Sail area	10,220 sq. feet
Engines	2 x 180 bhp petrol engines
Photograph date	1969
Photograph location	Antigua, West Indies

YOUNG AMERICA

Launched in 1975 as the *Enchantress,* this ferro-cement brigantine was intended as a charter vessel run by the Port Jefferson Packet Company Inc., of Long Island. They ran her for three years, when she attended the huge Tall Ships Parade off New York in 1976. She was sold in 1978 to the Young America Marine Education Society, of Atlantic City, New Jersey, to be used for sail training with the new name *Young America.*

Her classic and graceful lines lead many people to be astounded when they realize that she has a ferro-cement hull; this material has an undeserved dubious reputation because it has been misused by so many unskilled amateur boat-builders. She is probably the largest sailing vessel to be built with this material and is certainly the largest square-rigger of this construction in the USA.

Although her sail plan is traditional, she has the unusual feature of having her wooden yards fixed in height and thus needing no raising, and her sails are brailed in to the masts like curtains. *Young America* can carry up to twenty-four trainees or sixty-five day-passengers.

Based in the historic Gardner's Basin of Atlantic City, she sails the American eastern seaboard of New England in summer and Florida in winter. This picture of her was taken during Philadelphia's 300th anniversary of founding celebrations in 1982 when a fleet of Tall Ships sailed down the Delaware River and on to Newport, Rhode Island. *Young America* was crewed on this occasion by American Girl Scouts.

Name of vessel	Young America
Year launched	1975
Designer	Charles Wirtholz
Builder	David Kent, Point Jefferson, New York, USA
Current owner	Young America Marine Education Society, Atlantic City, New Jersey, USA
Current flag	United States of America
Rig	Two-masted brigantine
Construction	Ferro-cement
Length overall	130 feet
Length of hull	93 feet
Length waterline	73 feet
Beam	23.7 feet
Draught	9.5 feet
Tonnage	94.6 gross
Sail area	6,000 sq. feet
Engines	1 x 180 bhp General Motors 6-71 diesel
Photograph date	1982
Photograph location	Philadelphia, USA

ZEBU

Launched under the name of *Ziba*, she came off the stocks at the yard of A. B. Holms, Raa, Sweden, trading as a gaff ketch, and carried salt, timber and grain cargoes for thirty-four years, after which time she was sold to and Englishman for charter. She was re-rigged as a Bermudan ketch and given a large deck-house.

In 1978, now under the name *Zebu*, she was re-sold and took part in the 1980 Tall Ships Race in the Baltic and North Sea. Again sold, *Zebu* was purchased by Nick and Jane Broughton on the understanding from the organizer of Operation Drake that, if she was brought up to the Department of Transport standards, she would be chartered for a round the world expedition. The charter was confirmed in March 1983 and on 11 October 1984 she left London on the first leg of her four-year circumnavigation.

Zebu has a crew of twenty-four, her master Peter Masters, owners, and sixteen young 'Venturers', and is to be used for special oceanographic, diving and logistical projects. The new Operation Raleigh is a multi-phase, multi-disciplinary expedition organized by the Scientific Exploration Society and led by Col. J. N. Blashford Snell. The brigantine is expected back in October 1988.

Name of vessel	Zebu
Year launched	1938
Builder	A. B.Homs, Raa, Sweden
Current owner	Nick and Jane Broughton
Current flag	Great Britain
Rig	Brigantine
Construction	Wood
Length overall	102 feet
Length of hull	72 feet
Beam	20.2 feet
Draught	7.5 feet
Sail area	4,250 sq. feet
Engines	84 hp Gardner 6LW
Photograph date	1984
Photograph location	Cowes, England

— FULL-RIGGED SHIP —

Three or more masts, each having a complete set of square sails.

— BARQUE —

Three or more masts, each square-rigged except for the aft-mast which is
fore-&-aft rigged.

— BARQUENTINE —

Three or more masts, each fore-&-aft rigged except for the foremast
which is square-rigged.